ROMANCE
ROMANZE

Two Novellas

ALSO BY RONALD ALEXANDER

The Final Audit
Below 200
The War on Dogs

ROMANCE
ROMANZE

Two Novellas

Ronald Alexander

Hollyridge Press
Venice, California

Hollyridge Press
P.O. Box 2872
Venice, California 90294

Cover Art © Svetlana Privezentseva | Dreamstime.com
Author Photo by Cynthia Smalley
Cover and Design by Rio Smyth
Manufactured in the United States of America by Lightning Source

Publisher's Cataloging-In-Publication Data
(Prepared by The Donohue Group, Inc.)

Alexander, Ronald, 1942-
    Romance romanze : two novellas / Ronald Alexander.

    p. ; cm.

    Contents: Tilden and Dewey: a corporate romance – A Romanze for Martha.
    ISBN: 978-0-9843100-0-5

1. Love--Fiction 2. Sex in the workplace--Fiction. 3. Triangles (Interper-
sonal relations)--Fiction. 4. Gay men--Fiction. 5. Love stories. I. Title.

PS3551.L35755 R66 2009
813/.54   2009940304

15 14 13 12 11 10 09   10 9 8 7 6 5 4 3 2 1

For Jamie

I thanked him for his hospitality. We were always thanking him for that—I and the others.
—F. Scott Fitzgerald, *The Great Gatsby*

Contents

Tilden And Dewey: A Corporate Romance

TILDEN MISSES HIS CONNECTION at O'Hare International Airport after he spots her swooping, a peregrine falcon, around a corner in terminal number two. It is because of the three businessmen who trudge into the waiting area and take seats across from him, that he looks up from his book of critical theory.

They wear nearly identical gray pinstriped suits, red ties and white shirts, and each man totes a canvas suitcase and an oversized hanging garment bag. Tilden understands that while they appear to be simple clones of some higher business power, they are in reality in competition with each other. As friendly as they might appear—laughing at each other's jokes, ogling the same women and complimenting one another on a new pair of shoes or a haircut—each would not hesitate to betray his companions for personal advancement. It is simply a matter of incentive: when the position is important enough or the salary great enough or the office large enough, any one of them will break ranks. After all, the whole point of this carry-on luggage is to see who can vault off the plane and get to the taxi stand first, isn't it? They quarrel as to whether a certain staff member's resignation has been voluntary or forced and, as their voices grow discordant and their gestures exaggerated, Tilden looks down at the open text on his lap. This eccentric Frenchman could deconstruct their artless arguments in an instant.

He closes the book and notices her. He'd been used to seeing her in business dresses and heels, shorts and sneakers, nightgowns and slippers, but now from the rear there is not even a patch of her pale, blue flesh exposed. Her height and the slant of her head give her away. In her uniform, Dewey looks decorous— and Tilden decides—masculine.

This chance encounter, in Chicago of all cities, surprises him. He runs to catch up with her, and she tells him that she has just flown in from Miami. Then she laughs, removes her cap and tosses her head, as if her black hair still grazes the tops of her shoulders as it did when they decided, during an evening of bitter cold with snow swirling on Wacker Drive like dry ice and the wind gusting to forty miles an hour outside the opera house after a tedious and uninspired performance of *La Bohème*, not to marry.

"Do you ever hear from Zach?" says Tilden. He pictures him, engaged in conversation, puffed up and practically on tiptoes. Then he sees him cleaning his fingernails and regrets having mentioned his name: in some ways Zach is the person most responsible for their reluctant decision to go separate ways.

"Not once in five years," says Dewey, placing her hand on his arm. "Do you believe that?" Then she angles her head forward in a gesture which seems so typical of tall women and says, "How are you, Tilden? I mean you look terrific, but how are you really?"

"Fine," says Tilden, not mentioning that he has published a dozen short stories since starting his new career. When they were together she made a point of not reading fiction, preferring she said, to stick to reality—a reality which she found in scientific journals and technical manuals and aviation magazines. When it came to reading, the only thing they had in common was the latest issue of *National Geographic*. Were Tilden to mention even his most prestigious sale, to *Mugwump Review*, she would simply exaggerate the angle of her head, smile beneficently at him and change the subject.

"I'm flying 767's now," she says.

❧•❧

He saw her in the glass-enclosed conference room, unpacking boxes. She straightened, each arm cradling a load of books and papers, and glanced out through the glass as he passed, then she smiled and adjusted her grip—a movement which Tilden read as an invitation or call for assistance—so he turned, went around the corner and through the door and introduced himself as the newest member (the only member really, besides Zach) of the Planning Department. "Want to have lunch?" she said. He followed her to her desk, located just outside Zach's office.

At the restaurant she ordered the bottle of Chardonnay, but he proposed the toast: *To a career of great accomplishments at Lesser!* She laughed and began a sarcastic denunciation of the Lesser family, aiming her most scathing remarks at Zachary Taylor Lesser, the founder of the company, who still insisted on coming into the Northcreek headquarters every morning to issue memoranda.

Tilden agreed. He'd seen no less than a dozen in his first week; most of them cautioning employees not to leave the lights on or eat at their desks or park in the executive lot. The best, circulated throughout the company and personally signed, read: *I will be away from the office on Friday at 4:00 P.M. for tooth replacement.* Tilden had scratched out *tooth* and written in *brain* before tossing the memo in his waste can.

"How pompous," she said, meaning the company designation: *Lesser Learning Systems.*

"Really," said Tilden. "Using his name despite the irony. What are *lesser learning systems* anyway? Broken chalkboards and textbooks with missing pages?"

Then Dewey made disparaging remarks about the Midwest, specifically mentioning the pasture of cows she had passed as she drove west on Lake Street. She came from Albany. Tilden hadn't imagined that someone might actually consider Albany, New

York more sophisticated than Chicago, but he was so pleased at her interest in him and so charmed by the lilting quality of her laugh that he joined in despite, or perhaps because of, the stab of pain he felt in his groin.

☙•❧

During the better part of 1985 he thought about death. For no apparent reason except that he had spent the first ten years after college, ten boring years, going to and from work at Imperial Petroleum. Ten years of getting on and off of the El, in and out of the elevators, up to and down from the seventy-ninth floor of the Imperial headquarters, watching his co-workers get fatter and grayer and balder and more wrinkled and less interesting and more sedentary—and bitter. Ten years of listening to them discuss the latest episode of *L.A. Law* as if it were Proust. For a while, four years to be exact, with Dewey, he forgot about death and started to live.

Crowds swell around them as if every flight has been scheduled for the same time. People bump Tilden's luggage and graze his shoulders and he steps in toward Dewey so that the space they enclose becomes tighter and smaller. "Time for coffee?" she asks. Tilden's plane doesn't leave for another hour, and they make their way to the fast-food area.

He asks about her parents, and she asks about his mother. He tells her he's been to Ohio and is on his way back to Los Angeles. "Does she still have a Coke problem?" says Dewey.

"She has a heart problem," says Tilden. "Forty percent blockage in the anterior descending artery and patches of sixty percent in other areas."

Dewey looks at her coffee and, as if the cup has suddenly grown quite heavy, she uses both hands to lift it to her mouth.

She takes a sip and places it back on the table. She looks past him into the crowd. Tilden remembers how difficult it was for her to discuss serious matters. "Did you fly over Gruesome?" she says.

ᔓ•ᔓ

She rented the plane, a red and white, single-engine Commander, and had it fueled and ready when he arrived at the airport at nine A.M. "Welcome to Palwaukee International Airport," she said, checking his seat belt and securing the door. "Now ready for departure."

The morning flight to Ohio was pleasant and uneventful. The sun bright, the sky clear. Tilden's mother met them at the end of the field's only runway. She wore a flowered blouse and a pink, hand-painted organdy skirt with matching gloves and purse which she carried in the crook of her arm. She'd taught her morning Sunday school class but skipped the church service to meet them. Her red convertible was not only the sole Falcon Futura in the parking lot, but also the only car and her first words to Dewey were the ones Tilden had predicted, but most surely would not have written: "You're as tall and lovely as Tilden said."

His mother drove fast along Airport Road, past the tall, browning rows of corn, slowing to sixty as they passed the *Welcome to Piqway* sign at the city limits and then to fifty as they descended the hill into town. Tilden understood this recklessness as his mother's way of showing that life in a small town need not be dull.

He turned to look at Dewey in the back. She rested her left arm on the bonnet covering the retracted top and used her right to keep her hair out of her face. As she gazed up at the tree branches fanning out over the street, the corners of her mouth turned up in the genesis of a smile, and Tilden could see the reflection of clouds in her sunglasses.

"I made a big pitcher of sun tea," said Tilden's mother as the tires of the Falcon squeaked on the driveway asphalt. She pulled the emergency brake, a quick tug which indicated that she didn't intend to waste time during the afternoon visit. "A pilot," she said to Dewey. "Tilden, I don't believe you've ever gone out with a pilot, have you?" She led the way up the sidewalk through the yard and onto the back porch. While she grappled in her purse for the key, Tilden looked around the yard; the grass had gone to seed and the spot which had once enclosed her garden nourished dandelions and some strange, flowering weeds. His mother turned the key and threw her shoulder against the door to unseat it, then led them through the kitchen and dining room and onto the side porch. Plates of cellophane-wrapped cookies and breads had been arranged around the perimeter of the glass-topped, umbrella-covered table and in its center sat a pitcher of iced tea and a vase of daisies.

"You know I had developed quite a Coke problem," said Tilden's mother, and when she went inside, Dewey cocked her head. "You mother is so avant-garde. Cocaine here in Piqway," she said.

Tilden's mother returned with a photo album and placed it in Dewey's lap. "I was drinking a six-pack a day," she said. "So I switched to tea."

A breeze rustled the leaves of the red maple which shaded the porch. The three spent the afternoon nestled in the salmon-colored patio furniture that Tilden's mother had won at Elmer's department store in their spring raffle. Tilden let Dewey and his mother do most of the talking; he was content to watch as they leapt to agree with each other. He didn't bring many girls home and knew his mother was mentally planning a June wedding.

At four o'clock, when dark clouds appeared in the west, Dewey phoned for a weather report. Minutes later she appeared back on the porch. "We'd better go; the weather looks iffy."

By the time they entered the area over Grissom Air Force Base, the weather had turned squally and black. Rapid bursts of lightening illuminated the sky around the small plane like a strobe. Black, white, black, white. The plane plummeted several hundred feet then jerked level as if suspended from wires. Tilden tried to appear casual with his hands folded in his lap. Dewey had stopped smiling. The propeller bored through the blackness like a drill through pine.

Dewey was on the radio to Grissom requesting clearance for a change in altitude. The answer came back: *Maintain current altitude until further notice.* Lightening split the sky, hanging long enough for Tilden to trace its jagged course. Dewey gripped the controls.

"Hello Grissom. This is Commander-Six-Eight-November. Seven thousand feet. Requesting lower."

"Negative, Six-Eight-November. Maintain eight thousand."

"Grissom approach. Six-Eight-November. It's getting dicey up here. Request lower."

"Negative, Six-Eight-November. Maintain."

The plane bounced through the storm, and Tilden grunted aloud after a punishing jolt made it difficult for him to breathe. He couldn't make out the tip of the wing because it was shrouded in vapor and, the part he could see, flexed and flapped like the balsa wing of a model airplane. "So," he said to Dewey, "how long have you been flying?" and it occurred to him that this might have been something to have asked before buckling in beside her.

"Listen Gruesome, Commander-Six-Eight-November leaving eight thousand for four thousand," said Dewey, her voice full of authority and yet, Tilden decided, shrill.

"Roger," he heard through the static, "Six-Eight-November. Descend to two thousand feet."

At the new altitude the ride was smoother and the sky a lighter, safer shade of grey. The engine droned evenly. But Dewey didn't say anything, and Tilden thought his voice might crack off-key if he attempted to speak. When at last the wheels touched down at Palwaukee and they sped down the runway Dewey looked over at him.

"That was exciting," she said.

"Pour me a glass of champagne," said Tilden.

෨•ඥ

Each time she lifts her cup to take a drink of coffee, her ring, an amethyst the size of an eggplant encircled by diamond chips, catches the light. But she wears the ring on the fourth finger of her right hand. Her wedding ring finger is empty. There are many things he would like to know, but instead he asks about her schedule, how many consecutive days she works, how many days she has off, what routes she flies and if she likes the people with whom she works. He remembers a time when she insisted that pilots were dull, unintelligent humans, using an especially caustic tone for anyone who piloted helicopters—until she discovered that Zach had flown helicopters in Vietnam.

Tilden listens as Dewey discusses her recent adventures. She says that when she is out of uniform people often mistake her for a flight attendant—then her smile vanishes and, with a trace of anger, she adds that she sets them straight. Even now, Tilden is not sure what made her want to be a commercial pilot. To him it seems not so different from driving a Greyhound between St. Louis and Phoenix, or hauling a rig loaded with hogs into Memphis. The occupation seems to have more in common with these ordinary and monotonous tasks. And it isn't the money. He knows. Zach made her rich.

❀•❀

"We're going to bring this company into the twentieth century," said Zach. He leaned back and studied the nails of his left hand. Tilden watched while he meticulously cleaned, clipped and buffed his fingernails; the middle drawer of his desk contained an assortment of tools which he considered then selected, one-by-one, as precisely as a surgeon.

His grooming was otherwise impeccable too: his fine, brown hair was parted neatly on the right and trimmed to just above the ears; the cuffs of his shirt were starched and so white it was a wonder they didn't reflect the sun's light on the walls of his office; his suit and tie combination probably cost at least a thousand dollars, and looked as if they'd never been worn before. And Tilden suspected, might never be worn again.

Considering that the year 2000 was about ten years away, he thought perhaps it might be time to think about the twenty-first century, but he smiled and nodded at Zach. "It's a matter of survival," said Tilden.

"And as far as the old man is concerned," said Zach, "remember that you work for me. If he so much as says *boo* to you in the parking lot, I want to know about it. Understood?"

❀•❀

Dewey has finished her coffee, and Tilden slides back his chair. "My flight," he says, turning his wrist so that she can see his watch.

"Take a later one," she says, leaning forward on propped elbows.

"Oh, you know, with these super-saver fares—"

"Have dinner with me." And before he can think of what to say, she begins to reminisce: she laughs as she recalls her uncertainty about relocating to the Midwest; she smiles as she describes her excitement on spotting him through the conference room glass; she reaches over and takes his hands in hers when she says: "Remember Montgomery?"

≈ • ≈

"We must diversify if we are to survive," said Zach, pointing to Tilden's bar chart of projected revenues. Tilden sat at the table of burled walnut, peeking up occasionally from his papers to look around at the board members' faces. Why didn't they call it what it was? A family meeting. Every person on the board, everyone in the room (except for Tilden and Dewey) was a member of the Lesser family, and their unanimity a foregone conclusion: they always followed the patriarch's lead. As Zach had predicted, his father-in-law was the key; convincing him had always been the only obstacle. "I urge you to approve of Montgomery: television is the logical direction for our growth," said Zach. "Hit the lights, Tilden."

Wednesday night. Montgomery was a languid locale with stifling heat and high humidity and—except for the bartender and the two businessmen in the far corner—the three of them were the only ones in the hotel lounge. Zach decided to go up to his room and get some sleep, claiming to be *bushed* though to be sure there were no physical signs of his exhaustion. He had changed before dinner into a fresh, white shirt and different tie and there was not even a single wrinkle on his navy blue suit. He had shaved and his hair was neatly combed; he looked more like a man going into the office than one ready to retire for the night. He suggested as he stood next to their stools that they do the same. "We have a lot on our plate tomorrow," he said, inhaling deeply as if by displacing air he could grow taller.

"But Montgomery makes me delirious," said Dewey. She batted her eyelashes facetiously. "Let's have a nightcap." Zach declined, and after he left, Dewey suggested moving to a table out of the bartender's earshot.

"For the first time in my life I feel like I'm in the right place at the right time," she said. She sipped her drink and put it down on the cocktail napkin, adjusting the glass in the exact center as if to signal the sudden seriousness of her mood. "With Zach I'm more than a secretary."

Tilden managed a smile. "Well, he certainly seems to know what he wants," he said.

They finished their drinks and walked to the elevator and started up to their rooms. Hers was on the fourth floor, his the sixth, but when the bell rang and the doors slid open at four she asked him to walk her to her room. She reminded Tilden that they were in the Deep South: the possibility of some inbred boy with rotted stubs for teeth and a speech impediment, reeking of hog manure and lurking in the hall, was real—not idle fantasy. When they got to her door she had trouble with the key—a flat, credit-card-sized piece of plastic which had to be inserted in a slot until a green light came on, then withdrawn before the door could be opened. "The secret is to slide it in fast and then pull it straight out," said Tilden.

"I know," said Dewey, leaning seductively in the now-open doorway.

He practically leaped at her, but missed her mouth and ended up with part of her upper lip and the tip of her nose in his mouth. She laughed and kissed him back, a lingering, gin-soaked kiss. She asked him in and he accepted, but then he chose to leave before things could get out of control; he couldn't relax with their boss in the corner suite on the same floor.

His decision was smart, if not satisfying, for Zach phoned him in his room even before six-thirty the next morning. He wanted to meet before breakfast, he said, to go over the morning agenda at the station. And over coffee, with papers spread out before them, Zach cleared his throat and said: "You know we have a lot of work to do. It's important that the three of us maintain a professional working relationship." And before Tilden could think of how to respond, or if he should, Dewey appeared in the doorway of the restaurant and started over to the table.

∝•∝

"Don't you stay with the rest of the crew?" he says. He hands Dewey's bag to the driver and climbs into the cab after her.

"I don't like it out here. I like to be in the city; I prefer the Ambassador East. In New York I stay at the Plaza." She slides over next to him and leans in close. "Why are you sitting so far away?" she says.

"It's been five years," said Tilden. "I don't know anything about your life now—"

"Let's catch up at dinner. Geoffrey's?" She takes his hand and holds it, and he laughs at her suggestion. Her captain's hat rests in her lap.

The evening air is cool and he keeps the window cracked an inch despite the exhaust fumes that accompany rush hour. Some of the trees are starting to turn. None are still vividly green; all have at least a touch of yellow or orange and a few of the maples have turned a deep, wine red. He is turning too: in a week he'll be forty.

They spend most of the ride in silence, and when they come to the junction where the Kennedy joins the Edens, their progress slows. After a few minutes, after they've merged with the traffic, he watches as a rapid transit train emerges from the ground and speeds along beside them in the median. When the train slows nearing a station then stops beside the platform while the taxi maintains its speed, Tilden decides it is too stuffy in the cab and he opens his window completely. He almost envies the passengers on the train: they can get off if they want.

ॐ•ॐ

"Geoffrey's again?" said Tilden.

By the time he and Dewey arrived at the restaurant, Zach and Sonya were having drinks. Tilden saw them through the frost-framed window standing at the end of the bar, talking to Geoffrey—a slender man with thinning hair. He dressed in kilts for the holidays and greeted his most favored clients at the door with a hug and a seasonal joke.

A ritual. Zach always brought them here to celebrate. They'd come after completing each acquisition: the four TV stations in southern growth markets and the two AM-FM stations in Idaho; they'd come after closing the two warehouses: located in declining markets and vastly underutilized; they'd come after unveiling plans for a new computer order processing and shipping system: projected to cut delivery time in half; and they'd come after spinning off the unprofitable specialty publishing subsidiary: CCS, which stood for Cosmetology Correspondence Systems—a business that required a burdensome inventory of wigs and false eyelashes and press-on nails and tweezers as well as cases of items like hair spray and depilatories and face creams: old man Lesser had had a lifelong interest in beauty regimens; Tilden joked that he was a closet hairdresser.

Zach and Sonya, self-proclaimed experts on haute cuisine, considered Geoffrey something of a celebrity and were enthralled by his attention, but in truth, the restaurateur's wit had too much in common with the floury sauces that he employed.

"Remember," said Tilden, before opening the door, "we're late because I couldn't find your new apartment."

Dewey bent her head and pushed her lips into a pout. "Remember to keep your hands off me during dinner," she said.

Sonya beckoned to them as they came through the door. Tilden stomped the snow off of his shoes, helped Dewey with her coat, and then hung them on one of the emptier racks. "You just missed Geoffrey," said Sonya. She reached to touch the front of her blond, highlighted hair, which had been teased and lacquered into place; there was little chance though, if any, that individual hairs might stray.

Tilden preferred the long, loose quality of Dewey's hair. It was hair that had to be touched to be completely appreciated. He liked watching her sleep, on her stomach, head turned to the side, her shiny hair covering one eye and fanning out to cover her bare shoulders and back.

Sonya laughed. "Did you hear the one about Santa's black eye?"

"Don't tell me he laid the wrong doll under the tree?" said Tilden.

Sonya screwed her mouth. "You have heard it. Poo."

At the table Sonya spread her napkin across her legs and took Zach's menu out of his hands. "I have something to say first and it's intended for all of you." She pushed again at the front of her hair.

"Sonya thinks we talk too much shop," said Zach.

She was right. Not that her topics (television soap operas, Hollywood films and best-selling romance novels) would be any better. But in principle she was right. There was a new production of *The Grapes of Wrath* at the Steppenwolf, the Monet exhibit at the Art Institute—and for that matter, talking about the Blackhawks would have been an improvement. Tilden started to mention the Chicago Symphony Orchestra concert—he'd taken Dewey to a performance of Solti conducting Bruckner's Eighth—but he decided it would be too complicated. Zach or Sonya might ask with whom he had gone, and then he might reasonably be expected to say something about the mystery woman, and then they'd want to know if it was their first date, and if it wasn't, they'd want to know how long he'd been dating and—what did it matter?

"Let's all say something about ourselves that's not related to the office," said Sonya. "Tilden, what have you been up to lately?"

He looked hard at Sonya. She stared back. And so did Zach. Zach and Sonya stared expectantly at him. And Dewey stared too: eyes wide and laughing. She was good; at that moment he thought she should be an actress she was so good. *Tabula rasa.* His brain began to search. Two weekends ago, he and Dewey had driven to Lake Geneva to go snowmobiling; Wednesday night they'd gone to see the Christmas windows on Michigan Avenue; Friday night they went ice skating in Lincoln Park. They spent nearly every night together at her apartment.

"I went to see the Chicago Symphony," he said. "Last Saturday night."

"You're kidding," said Dewey. "I was at that concert. Where were you sitting?"

She smiled and her lips moved as if anticipating his response. He wanted to lean across the table and take her face in his hands and kiss her; he wanted to laugh out loud at her audacity. God, how he loved her.

"In the first balcony—"

"Sorry to interrupt, Tilden, but we do have a little business to attend to," said Zach. "Sorry, honey." He straightened in his chair and looked at Sonya, but he wasn't sorry. Tilden could see that he was angry.

The waiter brought over a bottle of champagne.

After all four glasses had been filled, Zach raised his. "To another prosperous year. I couldn't have done it without the three people at this table. Til, great job on CCS. Dewey, you're indefatigable. Honey, the new family room looks fabulous." Then Zach took a sip and put down his glass and told them that he was bumping up their salaries, by twenty-five percent. "You'll earn it, too," he said. "When you see what I have in store for us."

•

Dewey sits forward to tap the driver on the shoulder. "Take the Fullerton exit," she says, "and then down Lake Shore Drive." She leans back again and turns toward Tilden. "I thought it might be nice to go past by my old apartment."

They cross Clark Street and near the edge of Lincoln Park. Tilden looks up at the building's exterior. Nothing has changed. Had she expected it to? It wasn't like her to be so sentimental. The windows of what had once been her living room, on the sixth floor, are dark. He'd stood there so many times, in the floor-to-ceiling windows, looking out over the park. He watched the sun appear on the lake's horizon on those occasions when he couldn't sleep.

∾•∿

Friday evening and the park was full of people playing with their dogs. Tilden stood in his under shorts, watching, when a familiar car pulled into the driveway at the building entrance.

"Dewey," he said, "What the hell is Zach doing here?"

Dewey came out of the bedroom. She had showered and was wrapped in a pink, bath sheet. Tilden repeated what he had said. "You're kidding," she said and started at a leisured pace back to the bedroom.

Tilden began at once to gather articles of clothing from the living room floor. That's where they had started; technically they started on the sofa, but they moved almost at once to the floor. "Doesn't the man ever take a day off?" said Tilden, and then the phone rang. Two successive and urgent jangles, signaling that it was from the lobby. She answered, then looked at Tilden and nodded.

"No trouble at all," she said. "Give me ten minutes. I just got out of the shower." She hung up and dashed past Tilden standing in the bedroom door. "He came to drop off some papers."

Tilden pulled his tee shirt over his head. "Couldn't it wait?"

"Why don't you ask him?"

Tilden stepped into his loafers and picked up his dirty socks and deposited them in the bathroom hamper. Dewey had put on a skirt and blouse and was combing her wet hair. She opened a jar and began to apply lotion.

"You're putting on makeup?"

"It's moisturizer."

Then there was the sound of the knocker at the living room door. Zach's sense of ten minutes had always been more like two when it came to something that he wanted. Tilden stood behind the bedroom door and Dewey rushed past. She pulled the door closed behind her, but Tilden immediately reopened it—just a sliver of an opening so that he could hear. The space gave him a partial view of the living room too; if he moved his head back and forth he could observe most of the sofa and part of the coffee table. And if Zach came too close to the bedroom, Tilden could always hide in the walk-in closet.

He heard the low rumble of Zach's voice, the officious tone he adopted to convey the gravity of his pronouncements. As if he'd just emerged from a meeting of the United Nations Security Council, he said, "My apology for barging in," he said. "I've just come from our downtown lawyers." He dropped his voice a further register here, and all Tilden could hear was the rumble. If he got any lower, the windows would start to rattle.

Tilden looked through the slot. Zach sat on the arm of the sofa and put his briefcase on the coffee table and opened it. He handed a manila folder across the table. More rumbling. Tilden tried to bring Dewey into his field of vision, but was unable. Then he heard her ask if Zach wanted anything to drink. Was she crazy? Playing the good hostess at a time like this? She swept past the slot on her way to the kitchen.

Zach slid off the arm and onto the couch. He scanned the room, and Tilden stepped back as if by reflex when Zach's eyes hesitated at the bedroom door. Tilden counted to ten and peeked through the opening again. He had picked up the biography of Amelia Earhart, the one Tilden had given Dewey for her birthday, and was reading the flyleaf. Tilden was trying to remember his inscription when Dewey came back in with the beer, and Zach put down the book.

Tilden stood staring through the crack for half an hour while the two of them talked as casually as if at a cocktail party. Dewey didn't seem to mind at all. She laughed, and Zach laughed. Why didn't she put out a little plate of finger sandwiches and fluff the pillows on the couch for him? Turn on the TV too. It was about time for *Friday Night Baseball*, after all.

And the maddening part: they hardly talked about the contents of the manila folder, and when they did, Zach kept his voice low. "...multimedia...New York...due diligence..." The words came to Tilden like fossilized bone chips, mere fragments—not nearly enough to reconstruct the entire specimen. No, they talked instead about people at the office: *What was with Marie in Accounting? Were they winding her perms too tight?* And: *Who was picking out Jerry's clothes anyway? How about that green suit he'd worn on Thursday?* And: *What had his father-in-law been thinking when he hired Nancy? The woman had the I.Q. of a sea slug—and a body to match.* They laughed like kids with their pants down.

And then, as Zach got up to leave, he smiled and Dewey stepped into view. She stood close to him—a full head taller— and smiled back. Tilden could hardly believe it, but he heard it, louder and more clearly than anything he'd heard all evening: "You look beautiful without makeup," said Zach. "Really. I mean it. Beautiful." He tilted back his head and looked up at her, and she ran her fingers through her still-wet hair, as if she wished to give him an unobstructed look, and smiled again.

❧ • ☙

Their taxi heads up the ramp and onto Lake Shore Drive. They merge with southbound traffic and Tilden looks out the window. The lake is murky, green, and choppy, and joggers are already starting to dress in heavier clothes. After Zach left that time, Dewey wouldn't talk about the manila folder. She wasn't at liberty to, she said. She assured Tilden that it had nothing to do with him, but she refused to discuss the contents of the folder. And Saturday morning, while she was still in bed, he looked for it, with no success, concluding after an hour's search that she must have locked it in the desk in her study. He decides, as the cab veers right at the Oak Street exit, that he will immediately return to the airport.

The doorman opens Dewey's door and she steps onto the sidewalk, and when the driver goes around the back to open the trunk, Tilden asks him to wait. Dewey hasn't heard; she is acknowledging the doorman's effusive greeting: "Let me get that for you, Captain. Good to have you with us again, Captain. You've changed your hair, Captain." She opens her wallet and hands two twenties to the driver.

"It's alright, Dewey. I'll pay him; I'm going back to O'Hare," says Tilden.

"Don't be absurd, Tilden. We're going to have dinner."

"The last flight is at eleven," he says. "I'd like to be on it."

"We'll eat here. In the Pump Room. There's plenty of time," says Dewey. "Please. For me?"

"Who gave you that ring?" says Tilden.

"Aren't you silly. Come to dinner. Please."

There is an even greater scene inside. Bellmen swarm, desk clerks gush and nod, chamber maids practically curtsy in the corridors; one would think Jackie Cochran had landed at Meigs Field.

Tilden sits in the chair and opens his book, an anthology of short stories. He starts to stretch out on the bed (Dewey has gone into the bathroom to shower and change) but he decides it would be too difficult to concentrate in a prone position. It will be hard enough to concentrate sitting upright—with her nearby. But there is so much to read, so much to learn, so much lost time to compensate for. He should have majored in English; he should have studied Nineteenth Century British and American Literature; he should have tried for an MFA—not an MBA. He has considered using white-out to alter his degree. A swipe at the bottom, a touch at the top, and behold: the "B" is an "F." He can't wipe out those years at Imperial though. All of those years spent with men whose heroes were Alfred P. Sloan and J.P. Morgan and E.I. DuPont, not Schopenhauer or Nietzsche or Foucault. All those years spent with men like Zach. At least there is no chance of him knocking at the door now.

☜•☞

He found the first excuse he could to stop by Zach's office—he told Dewey he needed to talk to the boss about the cash flow projections for the radio group—but even then he had to wait until almost lunchtime because Zach was on the phone to New York. Something was going on, that was for sure. Tilden watched the telephone console on Dewey's desk and as soon as he saw the light go out on Zach's extension, he went to his office and stood in the doorway. He rapped lightly on the open door; Zach had swiveled around in his chair and was gazing out at the lawn, as if deep in thought. It was spring by the calendar, but the weather was winter-like—typical for Chicago in April.

"Hey, Til. What's up?"

"I'd like you to take a look at these projections before I pass them on the accountants."

"Sure. Put them here." He patted the stack of papers on his credenza. "This is my afternoon pile."

"What can I take off your hands?" said Tilden.

Zach regarded his credenza for a moment, then turned in his chair, leaned forward, and studied the various stacks on his desk. He didn't delegate well. He had to be coaxed.

"Well there is something...I've been waiting for the right time." And here he picked up a folder on the left, rear corner of his desk. "Familiarize yourself with this. It's quite confidential; don't discuss this with anyone." He averted his eyes and cleared his throat. "Dewey knows, of course."

How long Zach would have waited if he hadn't been pushed? He relied so much on outside accountants and downtown law firms and New York consultants. Was he going to start leaving Tilden out too? Didn't he trust anyone? Besides Dewey, of course.

"Sit down, Til. Take a peek."

Tilden read the file. They were going after a Baltimore-based educational toy concern: The Suzie-Sox Company; named after the founder's daughter. Blocks and pegs and puzzles and musical instruments and anatomically-correct dolls that peed and cried and lactated. But it was practically already arranged. Consultants had found the company, public accountants had computed the proper offering price, and lawyers had prepared the contract. It was a done deal. Except of course for the due-diligence. Tilden was to leave at once. He was to spend the next month in Baltimore.

"You're in charge, Til. See that we know about every wart on their ass. Go through the inventory and books with a flea comb if you have to. Stay on their bean counters like a cheap suit.

When we're ready to close, we'll lower our offer by a couple million." As he'd left the office, Zach had reminded him to call in.

He called in all right. Each and every morning. Dewey put him through immediately to Zach—when he was available. She didn't want Tilden to call her at the office. She couldn't talk freely, she said. The spring weather in Baltimore was gorgeous—far more pleasant than Chicago—but so what. Tilden was miserable. He might as well have been in a Siberian labor camp. He missed Dewey. He missed the scent of the powder she used after the bath she took before climbing into bed at night; he missed the peppermint smell of her breath; he missed the sweetness between her legs that lingered even after her shower. He dined alone each night, or worse, spent it in the company of accountants who spoke only of tax codes and proforma financial statements and Financial Accounting Standards Board pronouncements. As a cost-cutting measure, Zach suggested, strongly, that Tilden stay in Baltimore over the weekend too; that way he could work on Saturdays and get the job done sooner.

❧ • ☙

Does the Pump Room require gentlemen to wear ties? When Tilden realizes that he is staring at the bed, he immediately turns toward the window. Through the diaphanous sheers, he sees the Ambassador West. He parts the fabric and scans the façade of the sister hotel. The window directly across from this room is lit; a woman steps into view and glances down at the street, as if looking for someone or possibly wishing to forecast the evening weather in order to dress accordingly. The temperature often falls rapidly—and unexpectedly—in Chicago. He hasn't packed a heavy jacket and seldom wears a suit these days; he is wearing a sport coat, a concession to his mother who likes for him to escort her to church when he comes home, but he doesn't have a tie. He is about to call downstairs to ask, when Dewey comes out of the bathroom.

"Why so glum?" she says. She wears a black, mid-length dress, a worsted-wool blend he believes.

"That's a lovely dress," he says.

"A slip-dress," she says, and sits in the chair by the window. Perhaps he is fortunate that she has come out of the bathroom already dressed, that he hasn't had to watch. The only light in the room comes from the two ginger jar lamps on the end tables flanking the bed and the luminescence from the street that filters through the drapery sheers. The interior light has a pink tint to it, while the light cast from outside is yellow. Tilden sits on the edge of the bed, watching as she crosses her legs and pulls on her stockings. The two colors meet on her face at the bridge of her nose. There is something about this lighting and Dewey's oval face that reminds him of those Modigliani portraits of women with expressionless faces and elongated features. Dewey hasn't put on weight—if anything she is a little too thin, almost gaunt—and Tilden looks down at his stomach involuntarily. It has been a year now since he has had two consecutive dates with the same girl. He joined a gym for Stacy; he was in great shape then. But after she left for New York he quit jogging and lost interest in the treadmills and stair-climbing machines that were such an integral part of her life.

"Fasten me," says Dewey.

He goes to her. "I used to have to pull your hair out of the way," he says, as he hooks the clasp.

"Short hair is so much easier," she says. She stands, goes over to her luggage and takes out a pair of black heels.

"Pumps for the Pump Room," says Tilden.

"You look miserable. What's wrong?"

"I don't know if I'm dressed right," says Tilden.

"What's really wrong?"

"Remember when I came home from Baltimore that time?" he says.

Dewey pulls on the second shoe and straightens. In them, she is almost as tall as Tilden. Darkness clouds her face. "That's what you remember? Every disappointment."

⁕•⁖

He flew home early Friday afternoon and went to his apartment to check his mail and messages. He planned to shower and change and then get flowers and a bottle of champagne on the way to Dewey's place. The prospect of seeing her for the first time in four weeks excited him; he thought only of her, only of her touch. They had talked for nearly an hour the night before and she missed every bit as much as he missed her; she said she was dying for his pot roast and mashed potatoes and suggested that since he was getting home early, if he felt like cooking, she'd pick up something romantic at the video rental store and they could spend the night at home. There was no reason to leave the house; no reason to leave the bedroom for that matter she said, her voice as soft as kitten's fur. But that was Thursday night. Now, on Friday, as he played his messages, her voice was like a stranger's.

"It's Friday noon. I'm in Teeterborough, New Jersey," and after a long pause, "with Zach." Another pause. "I'll be home Saturday afternoon. I'll explain then. Don't worry. Nothing is wrong. Sorry about tonight. I love you."

Tilden felt like vomiting. His dreary apartment came into sharp focus: the cobwebs in the corners, the dead flies on the window sills. The place had been abandoned, like Pompeii and the ruins at Teotihuacán. He paced, he ate, he flipped through the television channels, he tried to read, and in desperation called a few old friends to see if anyone wanted to meet for a drink. Recorded messages were all he got. *Hi, It's Bob. I'm not in now…You have reached 969-7711…Sorry, I'm not here to take your call…*What with the demands of work and his relationship with Dewey—and the fact that he'd been in Maryland for a month—he had slipped from circulation, so much flotsam washed ashore. But he could deal with the boredom, the loneliness, the absence for one more night if not for the suspicion that something inconcinnate existed between Dewey and Zach. A part of him said it was his imagination: Dewey was the man's private secretary; her position called for, demanded, special ties. It was true Tilden and his mother had been abandoned by his father and that had left him scarred with insecurity (he still got nervous when he saw a suitcase being packed) but that was old news; he'd worked that out in therapy. No, the way Zach acted in Dewey's presence worried him: the change in his demeanor, the softening around his eyes, made Tilden suspicious. And that was a month ago, even before the trip to Teeterborough; there was no telling how things were now.

Tilden didn't hear from Dewey until nearly seven o'clock on Saturday night, when Zach dropped her off; she said she called the minute he left, but she wouldn't tell Tilden why they'd gone on the trip. It was business. She assured him that Zach would tell him first thing Monday morning.

She threw herself on him and kissed him hard the moment he walked through the door, but Tilden stood with his arms at his sides. She was positively feverish with excitement and this made her all the more alluring, and he wanted to be stronger, less troubled by the circumstances, but he couldn't help himself.

"I know for a fact that you're going to be involved in this, but it has to come from Zach," said Dewey. "Can't you see that? He's our boss. We're both very dependent on him. What would happen to us if we were out of work?"

"He's attracted to you," said Tilden.

"He's married," said Dewey. "You're being ridiculous."

"Are you attracted to him? You look ridiculous together."

And without answering she took his hand and pulled him into the bedroom and over to the bed and when she placed the palm of her hand on his chest and pushed, he allowed himself to fall back onto the bed. He lay there in his clothes and watched as she unbuttoned her blouse and stepped out of her skirt and underpants and stretched out on top of him. "You know perfectly well who, and what, I'm attracted to," she said, as she reached to unfasten his zipper.

∾•∿

Zach appeared in the doorway of Tilden's office. "Til, got a minute?"

Tilden looked up from his printout. So this was it, though it was hardly first thing Monday morning; his watch said eleven-thirty. Zach closed the door, approached the desk and sat across from Tilden. He watched as Zach's eyes shifted down to the printout. "How's that looking?" said Zach, nodding toward it and the other papers in the center of Tilden's desk. Did Evelyn Wood give seminars in upside down speed reading?

"With the interest we've been paying, income is down steeply." An understatement to say the least: nobody recommended buying Lesser Learning now and most of the bigger analysts had issued sell recommendations. They said Lesser had expanded too fast, had taken on too much, had become too burdened with debt. "In the last six months our price per share is down more than fifty percent," said Tilden.

"Don't show that to my father-in-law," said Zach.

Then, uncharacteristically, he leaned back, crossed his legs at the knee, unbuttoned his suit jacket and clasped his hands behind his head. He smiled, his mood suddenly bright as a sunflower at high noon. "Put everything else on hold, Tilden. I've got a hot one for you." He unclasped his hands and stretched his arms toward the ceiling. "We're going to get ourselves an aero plane," he said. Tilden leaned forward and nodded.

"Tell me more," said Tilden.

Dewey had shown Zach an ad in the *Wall Street Journal.* A company in the East was upgrading their corporate fleet and was selling a used Falcon-100. He and Dewey had gone to New Jersey to inspect it over the weekend and the old girl (the plane, not Dewey) was in fine shape—except for a minor oil leak in the number two engine—and looked like a damned good deal at only $1.4 million. They'd have to put a little something in it to bring it up to speed, so to speak, but when all was said and done they'd have themselves a fine investment. After all, one didn't justify such a purchase on the basis of cash outlay or cost comparisons with commercial flights or anything like that. If dollars were all that was important, they'd take the bus. No, it was about efficiency, the proper use of an executive's time; that's where the savings would accrue. That was Zach's pitch, more or less, replete with generalizations and clichés and gross simplification. And Tilden was in charge of the presentation to the board; he was to put the numbers together in such a way that their approval was a foregone conclusion.

"Oh, and one more thing," said Zach. "Dewey and I are going to fly her. I only need a few hours to get recurrent and after Dewey spends a few weeks in Teeterborough at FlightSafety, she'll be ready." He used both hands to smooth back his hair at the temples. "Wait till you ride in her, Til. She's a beaut." Tilden stared at him and forced a smile. Who did Zach think he was? The Sultan of Brunei.

∾•∾

Tilden looks at his watch. "We'd better get to the restaurant," he says. In the elevator she loops her arm through his and leans her head against him. If he brought up the plane now, Dewey would remind him that they had sold it for a profit. "Think about the exciting times," she says. "Nobody else ever took you skydiving."

There are more smiles and waves from hotel employees as they pass through the lobby and approach the steps to the Pump Room. The walls are covered with pictures of celebrities, a somewhat unusual practice in Chicago given its location in the middle of the country, though in Los Angeles every car dealership, every dry-cleaner, every veterinarian and every frozen yogurt shop have framed photos of one-time, little-known stars. Tilden starts to ask when Dewey's picture is to be hung, but instead points out the picture of the gossip columnist—the one who first mentioned the problems between Zach and Sonya. The photo has been so drastically retouched that all that remains of the real woman is platinum, bouffant hair, which swirls around her head like cotton candy, blackened eyes and two holes of a nose. "Isn't that what's-her-name?" says Tilden, putting his face close to the glass.

At the host stand a young girl is poised over the reservation book, pen in hand. She contorts her mouth, anguishing over seating arrangements or time slots or someone else's illegible handwriting. When she looks up and sees Dewey, she smiles, though not with the enthusiasm that the male employees of the hotel have exhibited. The girl, dressed in black, is perhaps twenty, attractive and slender. She is rather short (5'7" is considered short these days isn't it?), and Tilden suspects that she might be intimidated by Dewey.

An older woman—the hostess—greets them in a heavy, English accent and leads them down three steps into the dining room. "We've reserved Booth One for you," she says, sweeping her hand over it in a grand gesture.

"Quite elegant, I'm sure," says Dewey, affecting a cockney English accent. A waiter pulls out the table and waits for Tilden and Dewey to slide in and once they are settled, side by side with napkins on their laps, he pushes it back. "Look, Tilden," says Dewey. "They still have the telephone. Loverly."

"Oh yes," says the girl. "We have phones at Booth One, Two, and Three." She has either not caught Dewey's sarcasm, or chosen to ignore it.

"And it's so feminine," says Dewey. She runs her fingers over the top of the cradled receiver. The telephone, though touch tone, looks like something Louis XIV might have used (if they'd had telephones) as it is white and trimmed with filigreed gold. "Seems obsolete with everyone carrying their own these days," says Dewey. And then, in an abrupt movement, the way a canary suddenly decides to hop to another perch, she turns to Tilden and puts her hand on his shoulder. "Let's call Zach."

"Skydiving is a great metaphor for our relationship," says Tilden.

"Metaphor? You really are taking this writing business serious."

"Yes, I'm taking it very seriously," says Tilden.

"I'm not sure I know what you mean," says Dewey.

"My memories of Zach aren't as pleasant as yours. He fired me, remember? And you slept with him. What's happening here?" Dewey's smile disappears, and Tilden thinks her eyes mist slightly, but she looks away when the waiter appears with menus.

Tilden lowers his voice when the waiter leaves. "What's gone on in your life? Were you ever married? Are you married? Are you engaged? Are you happy?" And then it occurs to him that the amethyst might be a gaudy engagement ring. The prospect unexpectedly makes his own eyes mist over.

❧•❧

Tilden did not care for heights nor did he enjoy taking unnecessary risks. Skydiving seemed to be on everybody's agenda. At least that's what Dewey said. She opened magazines to show him pictures of people skydiving in formation; she called him to the television to see the ninety-year-old woman who had celebrated her birthday with a jump; she even joined in conversations with complete strangers at restaurants or in line for movies if she heard any mention of skydiving. And through it all he presented a sober and interested face, while inside he prayed for an act of Congress declaring skydiving illegal or a medical breakthrough that once and for all linked skydiving to prostate and breast cancer. But of course no such events transpired and then Sunday morning at the breakfast table over espresso and homemade cinnamon rolls which Tilden had baked from scratch (on Saturday night because the yeast needed time to expand the doughy mixture into a light, luxurious and fluffy masterpiece) she finally said it: "Let's go skydiving."

At first, Tilden tried honesty: "I'm not comfortable with the idea of jumping from an airplane."

"You should confront your fears; it will make you more aggressive."

First Zach sent Tilden away from Dewey to Baltimore, then he sent Dewey away to New Jersey. Tilden could not allow yet another separation no matter how brief. If he didn't jump with her, Zach probably would. If she wanted to leap from a plane and plunge to the ground he resolved to be there, beside her, not on the ground looking up.

They arrived in Sandwich, Illinois, a smatter of buildings just one hour and a half southwest of Chicago, and inquired about the airport—if one could call it that. It was nothing more than an air strip and Quonset hut along a country highway. An old DC-3 in need of paint, and who knew what else, rested on the tarmac; a small crowd had gathered near it. The barefoot man in charge, Glen, appeared unable to escape the seventies; he sported a scraggly beard, and his right cheek bulged with a wad of tobacco.

"It's good you're here; we start at eight," he said. "Soon as I get the cash. That'll be one hundred fifty each in advance." He withdrew a large wallet, tethered to his waist by a chain, from the front pocket of his coveralls and unzipped it expectantly.

Tilden surveyed the plane while he fumbled for his own wallet: he wore new khakis and had difficulty unbuttoning the flapped, rear pocket. Glen eyed him suspiciously and spit on the ground at Tilden's feet; he accepted the bills and counted them, not once but twice, and after he was apparently satisfied that it was all there, he handed a stack of forms to Tilden. There were eight in all (four for Dewey and four more for him) marked with red X's in the places where they were to be signed. Glen started toward the hanger, motioning for the others (about twenty people in all) to follow.

Dewey had already become friendly with another couple and she introduced them to Tilden. The man said he worked as a plumber but his real passion was competitive bodybuilding and, more recently, skydiving. He told Tilden that he and his girlfriend had made about a dozen jumps in the last three months.

Glen faced the jumpers now in the corner of the hanger. "We have a video for you and four hours of ground school before we break for lunch." He pointed to the opposite corner of the hanger. "That's my dad at the lunch counter. I myself recommend the breakfast burrito."

Tilden watched the video and listened to Glen assiduously, as if they were planning an invasion at Grenada, and the morning passed quickly. Too quickly for Tilden. Dewey had by now completely bonded with the plumber and girlfriend—their names were Max and Patricia—and Tilden merely nodded his assent when they suggested getting together for a movie and dinner later in the evening. Glen droned in the background, summing up his presentation, and then announced the noon break. He raised his voice to be heard over the buzz of the students, who had burst into excited and frenzied conversation among themselves, to push the breakfast burrito: "Don't let the name fool you; it's good for lunch too." Tilden decided to pass on lunch, though to his amazement, Dewey, Max and Patricia and the rest of the crowd ate eagerly. Max, in particular, sported a voracious appetite and bolted down no less than three burritos, two bran muffins, and two cartons of orange juice.

After lunch, they spent an hour jumping off of a ten or twelve-foot-high platform to practice landings, and they were instructed on the proper way to deploy the parachute—and a small emergency chute in case the main one failed to open. Tilden's mouth was dry and he had an insistent urge to urinate because he had postponed a trip to the men's room for several hours now, for fear of missing some vital piece of information that might impact unfavorably on his impending jump. He glanced at his watch; it was two o'clock: time for takeoff.

The plane bounced down the runway, engines roaring. Max was to jump alongside him; he sat in front of Tilden closer to the door. Tilden felt small and inadequate, almost feminine, next to the behemoth: with the parachute pack and gear he reminded Tilden of the Michelin Man. "How are you doing, buddy?" said Max, patting him on the arm, perhaps overwhelmed by the miasma of Tilden's fear. Dewey sat on the other side of Tilden and she took his hand and clasped it and smiled at him. He could feel the vibration of the plane against his back and throughout his body. The vibration decreased, but did not stop, as the wheels left the ground.

As the plane gained altitude, Glen shouted last minute reminders from his position on the opposite wall of the plane. "Arch. Reach. Look. Pull." Tilden could not believe he was doing this. Sheer insanity. Events were happening in slow motion now: Jesus, he hadn't even jumped and his body was in shock. Max's hand took hold of his arm and lifted him. Tilden stood at the open door flanked by Glen and Max. The sun shone, brilliant and beautiful, and Glen shouted that there was not even the whisper of a breeze—nothing that might cause a last-minute reprieve—and Tilden remembered now a story of jumpers being blown off-course and into high-tension power lines. His legs wobbled, almost unable to support his weight, as if Max had suddenly straddled his shoulders for the ride down.

Framed in the doorway Tilden surveyed the countryside. Farmland surrounded them all sides. What were they going to land in? Clover? He'd forgotten to ask. And when he stepped into space—There'd been a hand on his back; had Dewey pushed him?—he realized that he had forgotten to say goodbye to his mother.

When he did talk to his mother, when he told her what he'd done, she said she wanted to make a jump too; when he told her how at first there was no sensation of movement, how he checked his altimeter, how he pulled the cord, how he guided his descent, tugging left then right on the straps of the parachute, she clasped her hands together in wonderment; when he told her how the wind felt on his face, how all the blood in his body seemed concentrated in his head, how it was as if he'd been injected with a drug, she put her hands to her cheeks, suddenly flushed with color; when he told her how he laughed and giggled the rest of the night, how he couldn't stop talking, how he had hugged Dewey, and Patricia and Max too, how he had thrown his arms around the beast and laughed as if they'd been in the trenches together at Verdun, she had reached out and touched his face and smiled as if single-handed he had saved an entire family from a burning tenement. Of course, he didn't tell her how he had landed on his backside, how Dewey and the others had landed upright, in a standing position. It was a wonder she hadn't worn heels. No, he hadn't revealed this sordid detail to his mother. Dewey did that for him. "It was adorable, Mrs. Scott," she said. "You should have seen him. He looked so cute sitting there, all wide-eyed and smiling."

He didn't tell his mother either that, for an instant lasting no longer than a footprint in a dust storm, he had considered not opening the chute.

&⚬&

Dewey closes her menu, glances at the telephone for a moment, as if she might actually make a call, then she looks up at

Tilden. "I'm married," she says. She holds his gaze, and Tilden realizes suddenly that she looks quite tired. The muscles around her eyes have relaxed for the first time.

"Well, that's good. Isn't it?" says Tilden.

And here, he decides that she is sad. He doesn't know if it is because she has not wanted to hurt him or if there is some problem with her marriage. Whatever. The fact is that the absence of a wedding ring has led him to a mistaken conclusion, and he regrets having forced the issue. There are times when his writing—the mere thought of himself as a writer—provides consolation, a refuge of sorts. He needs something now to distract him from this unexpected and unwarranted emotional setback. But he hasn't had a story accepted in over eighteen months.

The waiter appears once again and asks if they are ready. Tilden hears Dewey order the tournedos of beef tenderloin while he contemplates the menu; it might as well be a listing of credits for a Japanese film. The space around them has grown suddenly small. His eyes pass over the type—up and down and from one page to the other—and when he hears the attendant's impatient exhale, Tilden points to an item. "Ah, the Duck," says the waiter.

Dewey angles her head and reaches for a piece of bread. "He's an environmental attorney; his name is Brad; we live in Dallas. We met when I was working for a charter outfit down there. I have a little girl: Daisy. She's three." She tears the bread in half and looks at Tilden and smiles. "What about you, Tilden?"

What about him? He rents a one bedroom in Venice, a block from the ocean, which he never swims in because the water isn't clean enough (there was a cholera outbreak in Malibu of all places), and there is no one in his life and he has few friends and the ones he does have don't understand why he doesn't write screenplays or teleplays because: *That's where the real money is.*

Given the lack of material evidence, it would be impossible to tell her how much he loves his life or that he anticipates each day with an optimism which for him is unprecedented. She wouldn't believe that he lives an utterly privileged, utterly luxurious existence. But he does. Tilden can't wait for the sun to come up in the morning and often doesn't, sitting at his computer in the dawn to work on his novel, and he can't even concentrate at the movies anymore because he keeps thinking about his own work, and sometimes he has to force himself to leave his desk and walk on the beach just to clear his head. This woman couldn't understand the beauty of a well-crafted paragraph or the joy of rhythmic, musical prose or the contentment one derives from living as an artist. It would be impossible to make her understand. Writing fills the emptiness. Writing gives his life purpose.

If she married a year before her daughter was born, that meant she married just one year after they split up, that meant she probably met him, this Brad, a mere six months or less after he and Dewey had parted. An instinct deep inside tells him to get up from the table and run from the restaurant. Run before she sees. Run. So much for broken hearts. Apparently Dewey would always land on her feet.

ॐ•ॐ

After she got certified to fly the Falcon-100, Dewey talked of little else. Tilden had presented the numbers to the board and made them work and to his amazement Ole Man Lesser showed less resistance than on any of the company acquisitions. But that was the last time Zach had his father-in-law's cooperation for anything. He had managed to have his own way with the acquisitions by allowing the deluded man to have much of, if not all of, the credit. When things were going good and there were daily doses of publicity in the *Chicago Tribune* and the *Wall Street Journal* and the *New York Times*, Zach made sure his father-in-law took the credit. *I am guided by Zachary Taylor's inspiration. He wants a more profitable, more diversified company for our stockholders. To others he may be a hard-driving, taciturn executive, but to me he's a man with a vision. My job is to realize his vision.* "And you can quote me," said Zach.

Zach even planned a tour of the new company operations for Ole Man Lesser. Like Rasputin, Zach cajoled, coaxed and flattered: "You're the man who built this firm and you're the one who grew it," he said. "You owe it to your employees, especially the television people who appreciate charisma, to let them get to know you." Zachary Taylor Lesser's eyes were milky blue and brimming with emotion in the face of these remarks. There was the slick and shifty quality of the mountebank in Zach's performance, and Tilden wondered why the old man didn't see it. Had he slowed down to such an extent that the constant flurry of activity and acquisitions had left him dazed and dizzy and bewildered?

One day, the old man calculated the value of his holdings at current market prices. His wealth, on paper, had been halved and try as Zach might (he brought Tilden in to help) he could not convince the man that the lowered price was a temporary phenomenon owing to the decrease in short term earnings.

Afterwards Zach and Dewey started making the trips to New York: three separate ones during November alone. Needless to say, Dewey couldn't discuss the nature of their business so Tilden stayed back in Northcreek and tried to concentrate on the prosaic projects which Zach left for him. He walked past Zach's darkened office, he stood in front of Dewey's clean desk, he looked in the empty conference room. He took strolls around the grounds to pass the time. He left the executive floor and wandered the corridors of the complex of buildings—set apart to the rear—where the real work was done. Here were the former teachers and educators and designers who conceived of and produced the Lesser Learning tools; here were the people who packaged them and sold them to the schools; here were the people who talked to manufacturers and arranged for the shipments to and from the warehouses; here were the people chose colors and typefaces, people who talked to children, people who cared about others, people who were involved in actually making something of value for the world. They didn't simply live for numbers; they didn't just dream of bigger profits and more employees and faster turnover and higher margins and an increase in the return on their investment. They weren't interested in building an empire. But Zach was. Oh, yes. He was determined. Rupert Murdoch? Ted Turner? Donald Trump? Who were they? He was going to be bigger than all of them. And Dewey was with him. More and more. She didn't just agree with him. She adored him. She couldn't speak highly enough of him, couldn't seem to speak of anything else really.

Tilden stuffed his running shoes in the bag and was checking the front hall closet to make sure he hadn't left any of his clothes when he heard the key in the lock. He looked at Dewey's grandfather clock in the entryway: *Ten past four.* She'd arrived home early.

The door opened. "Oh," she said. "I called you at the office. Nancy said you'd already signed out." Then Dewey glanced at the duffel bags and boxes. "Going somewhere?"

"Home," said Tilden.

"Any particular reason?"

"One—in particular," said Tilden.

"I see," said Dewey.

"Well, bye," said Tilden. He picked up the larger of the two duffel bags. Dewey leaned against the door.

"Can't we talk about this?"

"Not right now. Could you get the door for me?" She stepped aside and allowed him to pass. He told her he'd be back to get the boxes and that he'd call her over the weekend, but when he came back up to get them, she'd gone into the bedroom and closed the door.

That night he went out to a few of the bars on Division Street. The crowd seemed so much younger and everyone gathered in cliques as if they already knew one another. It was as if he'd been invited to a party given by strangers. Tilden stood at the end of the bar and spent most of the evening looking out through the window at the falling snow, but no matter where he looked or what he saw, he thought of Dewey. Christmas was a few weeks away, and he didn't look forward to spending the holidays alone.

He was still in bed, with a headache, when the phone rang on Saturday morning a little before nine. "Can I take you to breakfast?" said Dewey.

He found a parking spot on a street which led through Lincoln Park and walked across the snow covered grass to meet her at Un Gran Cafe. Inside he saw her at a corner table.

He took off his coat and draped it over the back of his chair and sat down. Dewey smiled and straightened in her chair. "I missed you last night," she said.

"I need coffee," said Tilden.

He turned, waited until he caught the busboy's attention and held up his cup. The boy nodded and came over. While he poured, Dewey and Tilden watched in a motionless hush, as if the slightest noise or movement would distract the man from this important scientific experiment. After he had topped off the cup and dropped a handful of the thimble-sized, half-and-half containers in the center of the table and left, Tilden and Dewey looked at each other.

"I was—" they said in unison.

"What?" said Dewey.

"No, go ahead," said Tilden.

"No, you," said Dewey.

"Breakfast was your idea," said Tilden.

"Moving out was yours," said Dewey.

Tilden bit the inside of his upper lip and cleared his throat. Whenever he drank too much, in a bar, he noticed that the following day his throat tended to clog with phlegm and his voice came from a deeper place inside his chest. He attributed it partly to the effects of the alcohol, but more to the blue gray smoke, that curled through the air like mustard gas.

"I love you," he said at last, "but this is not working." And then he spilled it. He told her how lonely he was when she was gone, how bored he was at work with the tedious and routine assignments that Zach dribbled out for him, how left out he had become, how unimportant and overlooked he felt. He admitted that he was bitter and resentful, that he had trouble even looking at Zach these days because he had never done anything but his best work for the man and it wasn't fair that a person should be so wasted. And yes, Tilden confessed that he suspected her of being unfaithful, that he couldn't stand seeing her fawn over Zach as if he were third in line for the throne of England. Tilden said that he had decided his only chance for sanity and peace of mind was to break up with her and that on Monday, even though it went against everything he'd been taught, even though it was contrary to the advice of the headhunters, he was giving Zach his two-week notice.

She paused for a sip of coffee and then to send the waiter away. She said that she agreed completely with every single word of what he'd said, except for one thing: *There was nothing sexual between her and Zach.* Yes, she admired him. He made things happen. He was proactive, not reactive. And she begged Tilden not to do anything rash. She knew for certain that Zach had nothing but the utmost respect for Tilden and she would talk to him on Monday. Something big was happening and Zach needed Tilden. She would definitely talk to him without giving anything away.

"The best is yet to come," she said. "Please come home."

☙•❧

Tilden mulls over the plate which the waiter has set before him. He doesn't care for duck. The only time he ever ate duck was when Sonya served it at her dinner party. Tilden spears a slice, tries to adopt a casual tone.

"So, your marriage is happy?" he says, and puts the piece in his mouth.

"You're going to have to help me with this," she says, staring at her own plate. "This is much too large a serving."

"I'll be lucky to finish my own," says Tilden. "This Brad, is he a good father?" This time his voice quavers slightly at the word *father*.

"He's a lawyer, Tilden. He doesn't have a lot of time to spend on his parenting skills." So much for his first question.

"But you said he was an environmental lawyer; at least he has a conscience, right? He cares about spotted owls and giant sequoias, right?"

That Lesser's business was *education* hadn't interested Zach. It had simply been a way to make money, a theater in which to wield power. For all Zach had cared Lesser might as well have manufactured assault weapons and landmines.

"Well, Brad's intentions are good, I think. Mostly he works for the government..." Then Dewey launches into a discussion of the problems with the profession of law. How competitive attorneys are, how controlling, how everything is a game, a game that has to be won, a game that, in the final analysis after all of us are dead and gone, won't matter. "It's all so egocentric and male-oriented," she says.

My God, how Dewey has changed. Of course it's about power. Lawyers are coyotes urinating to mark their territory. Tilden could have written her lines for her. He's heard these remarks about attorneys before. He has said them—and he believes them. But to hear them from her?

Dewey holds her knife and fork tightly and hunches forward over her plate. She turns to him and smiles. "It's an okay marriage. And he's absolutely devoted to Daisy. Would you like to see her picture?"

She puts down her silver and pushes away her plate; she has taken at most two bites of meat and a forkful of pureed carrots. She opens her black, leather purse and pulls out a small, matching wallet. She unsnaps it and flips through the plastic, photo section until she comes to a recent shot of Daisy, then hands the wallet to Tilden. Daisy sits in a pile of autumn leaves, unsmiling, staring solemnly into the camera; she holds a forefinger—the nail is covered with chipped, red polish—alongside her mouth. Daisy's hair is black like Dewey's; the curls evidently come from her father. Tilden turns to the next picture and ponders the photograph of the man whom he assumes is Brad. It is a formal photograph like one appearing in an annual report or hanging in a corporate headquarters; Brad wears a coat and tie, his wavy hair is neatly combed and parted on the side. Something about the picture reminds Tilden of Zach, but there is no real physical resemblance. Tilden decides that it's the pose.

"Brad?" says Tilden.

"Umm," says Dewey.

"Daisy is beautiful," says Tilden. "She looks like you."

Dewey smiles, and Tilden flips to the next picture. It is a shot of him, in a parka and Cubs baseball cap, at the outdoor ice skating rink at Rockefeller Center in New York.

❧•❦

Tilden looked through the undersized round window, down at the eastern shore of Lake Michigan. He watched the pattern of white caps on the water's surface for a while, then sat back in the rear most seat of the plane to study the contents of the manila folder which Zach had given him. The takeoff had been thrilling. Dewey told him the Falcon was basically the same plane as the French fighter Mirage—adapted though for the commercial market—and it had taken the jet less than a minute to leave the ground in a steep, swift ascent. Tilden studied the airplane's interior—the leather upholstery, the mahogany trim, the configuration of seating—and understood how easily one could be seduced by the allure of executive perquisites. The craft seated eight comfortably, yet he was the only passenger, except for Zach and Dewey who sat at the controls.

The door to the cockpit opened; Zach entered the cabin. He adjusted his cuff links and smoothed his tie and walked back toward Tilden. There was not a great deal of headroom, but Zach could walk without stooping. It was an illusion, for sure, but in this environment he almost appeared tall. He sat in the seat facing Tilden.

"This is it, Til," said Zach. He gestured toward the folder, opened in Tilden's lap. "We're taking the company private. We're making a tender offer for all the outstanding shares."

Tilden listened while Zach summarized. The New York investment banking firm, Barton, Endres, & Associates, would invest $500 Million to acquire the shares of Lesser: a fair price for the stockholders and a good deal for the investors—who would get a learning materials and educational publishing company, four television stations, two radio stations, and Suzie-Sox Baltimore. Since they were offering nearly twice the current per-share-price, Zach anticipated no problem in getting shareholders' approval. Zach had already spoken to his father-in-law and offered him a sizeable stake in the new private company. If he chose to be part of the new group (to be known as Lesser Limited), fine. If not, fine. Now the firm would be free to grow and invest for the future without the hassles and pressures of the industry analysts who only cared about short term earnings and quarterly reports. These people had no sense of the long haul. Zach was assured the support of the rest of the family board members; not only would they get twice what their shares were now worth but they would become partners in the new concern as well. Naturally, Zach would be President and Chief Operating Officer in the new partnership. Barton, Endres would not be involved on a day-to-day basis.

"And Til," said Zach.

"Yes."

"You'll be a partner too."

"I will?"

"I'm very proud of the job you've done."

"Thank you."

"But it means you'll even have to work harder."

"Yes."

"You'll have to work smarter too. Not just harder."

"Yes."

"And even if you get the avian flu or come down with pneumonia…"

"Yes?"

"You'll have to play hurt."

Then Zach went back to take over the controls, and Dewey came out. She poured Tilden coffee. He accepted the cup, and she sat next to him.

"See how nicely things are working out," she said. She ran her fingers along his jaw and over his lips. "You have such a nice profile," she said. "Zach can't leave the front. Feel like a quickie?"

"You're funny," said Tilden.

The plane landed in Teeterborough, and the three of them stepped into the waiting limousine and sped into the city with the urgency of Gorbachev on his way to United Nations Headquarters. And for three days, Tilden attended all the meetings: the breakfast meetings, the morning meetings, the luncheon meetings, the afternoon meetings, the dinner meetings and the after-dinner meetings in the Oak Terrace Room of the Plaza Hotel. They met among themselves—to discuss task assignments and to set deadlines—and they met with John Barton, Joseph Endres, and their staff—to discuss financing details. The snow started falling at noon on Friday as they were on their way to the Cote Basque for lunch.

It was one of those winter storms, when cold air from the north collides with warm from the south and the mixture sweeps unexpected up the Atlantic Coast gathering force and intensity on the way. By late afternoon the airports were closed and the city lay beneath four feet of wet, thick snow. And a marvelous thing happened. Zach disappeared.

"Can you two manage dinner without me tonight?" he said, glancing at his watch and adjusting a cuff. "I'll check in with you in the morning." But he didn't check in, and he didn't answer their phone calls to his suite either, and it was the last they heard from him until Sunday afternoon when the airports reopened.

Tilden stretched across Dewey's bed and opened the *Times* to the "Arts and Leisure" section. She called from the bathroom to suggest a movie or a play, but when Tilden saw the small ad for the Philharmonic concert at Lincoln Center he picked up the phone and called the box office. There were plenty of seats available; many of the subscribers were unable to attend owing to the extreme weather.

They sat in the center of the fifth row. Michael Tilson Thomas conducted: the first half of the concert consisted of music by Leonard Bernstein (Tilden had always loved *Candide*), and just before the intermission, the man himself, Lenny, came on stage to be named Conductor Emeritus of the New York Philharmonic. It was not only an extraordinary concert, but also high theater. Bernstein was predictably overwrought and teary-eyed and Tilden himself had fullness in his throat which he hid from Dewey by remaining silent until they went into the fore-court at the intermission.

"Not a moment too soon," said Dewey. "We were about to be swept away by the man's tears."

❧ • ☙

He hands back the photos and takes a bite of duck. She's done it again. The woman thrives on secrets. Why has she waited so long to let him in on her present life?

"I suppose I should have told you sooner that I was married," says Dewey. Tilden looks up suddenly from his plate.

There had always been that connection between them, that silent communication. "I suppose I was afraid you wouldn't want to spend any time with me."

"Why is it so important to spend time with me?"

"We were friends, Tilden. We were in love."

Tilden puts down his silverware, sits back and looks out from the booth into the restaurant. At the nearest table, a woman watches them—has been watching he realizes ever since he and Dewey were seated—as if puzzled about the identity of these people who rate Booth One. Tilden stares without blinking at the woman until at last she averts her eyes to take a sip of wine.

Dewey, still hunched forward over the table's edge, flexes the fingers of her right hand. "I know," she says, "I'm the dispassionate one." She begins to massage the muscle in her right forearm with her left hand.

It wasn't so much her lack of sentimentality that had disturbed him. He could have accepted that. But she accused him of being mawkish. Simply because he remembered their anniversary (March fifteenth) and brought her flowers; simply because he told her nightly that he loved her (*Have I told you I love you today?*) and kissed her on the cheek; simply because he wanted to be with her twenty-four hours a day.

"Wouldn't it be wild to see Sonya walk past our table right now?" says Dewey. "She was always so impressed with this place, especially Booth One."

"That kind of coincidence only happens in Dickens' novels," says Tilden.

Dewey smiles. "Excuse me, honey. I need to go to the Little Girls' Room." Tilden watches her until she disappears from view.

෨•ඏ

After the old man departed, Zach took his corner office and moved Tilden into the one he used to occupy. He gave Tilden a new title too: *Internal Consultant and Director of Strategic Configuration*. Things improved too. Tilden was involved. Or so he thought at the time. He wasn't sure whether Zach had been proactive or reactive. Had it been his plan to take the company private from the beginning or had he simply seen an opportunity when the share price declined? But the price had declined after he made all of the acquisitions, hadn't it? Maybe it was all by design. All of it. Maybe contacting Barton, Endres & Associates was step one. Maybe step one was Zach going to New York and saying to them: *Help me steal this company; help me screw my father-in-law*. That's what Sonya thought. She said so that day.

At first Tilden thought he imagined the noises coming from Zach's office. It was just thunder from the storm. Zach was gone. He and Dewey were on another week-long trip on the company plane. Tilden wasn't even sure where all they were going. Dewey had called in from Montgomery and then later from Idaho and most recently from New York. Then there was a thud against the wall. It wasn't thunder. It might be the cleaning woman. Was it that late?

He padded across the carpet, past Dewey's desk and stood outside Zach's doorway. Lightning flashed, illuminating a figure in black. Tilden reached around, fumbled for the light switch, flipped it on, and stepped inside.

Sonya gave him a perverse smile and turned off her flashlight. Zach's desk drawers had all been pulled open. Papers and binders littered the floor.

"I have every right," she said. "I used to play under this desk."

Tilden stood in stupefied silence. Rain splashed against the floor-to-ceiling windows. Sonya wore black. Black, spiked boots, a black raincoat, even a black, oversized, knit cap, pulled down to cover her blond hair, pulled down to cover her ears. Grease under the eyes would have been the finishing touch.

"Don't you care about Dewey?" said Sonya. Don't you care about her and my husband? Don't look so baffled. Everyone sees you, moping over her, like some love-sick cow."

෨•෨

Tilden looks up from the table. Dewey stands in front of the booth. "I've taken care of the check. Can we go upstairs?"

Tilden closes the hotel room door behind them. Dewey takes off her shoes and stretches out across the bed. He sits in the chair facing her and leans forward. "I really do need to get back to the airport," he says. Dewey nods.

"You were right, you know," she says.

"About?"

"Everything." She props the pillows behind her, filling the small of her back, and sits up a little so that her neck and shoulders rest against the headboard. "The shares you owned were worth ten times what he paid you for them. He got a phony appraisal."

Tilden gets up and walks to the bathroom and takes a handful of tissue to blow his nose. The air in the room has no moisture. That's the problem. Whenever the temperature drops outside in Chicago, the humidity drops inside. Moisture is being pulled from the air, from the joints of furniture, from the walls themselves—and from his body. His skin is drying, flaking off even while he stands there in front of the mirror. Every part of him is withering: his hair, his sinuses, his mouth. He takes a glass and turns on the cold water. He drinks a glassful then refills it.

"Tilden? Are you alright?"

He steps back into the room. "Sure."

"You said that Zach was a sociopath. Do you really think he was? Or is?"

Tilden takes a long drink, walks over to the bed, and sets the empty glass on the lamp table. "I don't know enough about psychology to say."

The fact is, the more he writes, the more he thinks he doesn't know much of anything. He doesn't know enough about psychology or philosophy or the Bible or Islam or Plato or Faulkner, and he doesn't have that great of a vocabulary either. He doesn't use words like hermeneutics and hegemony and sophism and ontology. Okay, so he knows about them, but he doesn't use them. And sometimes he has to look up ontology: he keeps forgetting what it means.

"Zach doesn't have much of a conscience. He's too self-involved to really care for others." He looks down at Dewey. "But then he did pretty well by you."

"It cost me," she says. "It cost me *you*."

"I'm not sure we can blame him for that, and besides, your life seems pretty good to me." Tilden looks at his watch. "I've got to go."

He sits on the bed next to her. Dewey's arms are folded across her stomach. Tilden puts his hand on her shoulder, then her neck. There was a place, just under the jaw line, where he'd always been able to feel her pulse, and he searches for it momentarily with his fingers before sliding them down to grip her throat in the web of his hand. She has such a long neck. He touches the front of her dress, cups his palms over her breasts, and moves down along the sides of her hips. When he finally looks into her eyes, they are filled with tears. Her hips protrude. Aren't women supposed to put on weight after having children?

She puts her arms around him, pulls him to her and they kiss. Her breathing is heavier, but he can tell she is trying to conceal the full extent of her arousal. It is an awkward position: he is still seated, twisted at the waist, head bent to reach her face. He sits up, turns, and starts to lie on top of her. "No," she says. "Not like this. Stay the night. My flight isn't till ten-thirty-five."

∾•∾

She pulled him down. He ran his hand up her arms and over her bare breasts and they kissed. Her skin was cool from the outside cold and covered with goose flesh. He pushed against her, thrusting with his hips, but she kept her legs together until he reached down with both hands to pry her apart, taking hold of her legs just behind the knees and lifting. She arched her neck and closed her eyes and he made a sudden, deeper thrust as he considered his anger. The bed's frame began to squeak and the headboard tapped rhythmically against the dry-walled partition. Dewey moaned. A sign that, at least for the moment, she was relinquishing any pretense of control. Tilden had gone to a poetry reading a few nights earlier; one large balding man, dressed in black, read a poem about fucking a girl until she screamed. The poet talked about pounding the girl until she was like *tenderized meat,* and he had used words like *friction* and *bone* and *cunt* and *cock* and *balls.* The poem had embarrassed Tilden, but thinking about it now increased his excitement.

After they finished Dewey sat at Tilden's desk and looked out through the basement window at the frozen ground. She had complained bitterly when Tilden took the apartment, but lately she had been spending the weekends with him and, although she still made sniping remarks about the industrial heater that hung from the ceiling and the roaches that ran for cover when she turned on the kitchen light and the metal shower stall that barely accommodated a normal-sized adult let alone someone as tall as she, he knew she enjoyed being there. "I'm going to plant flowers in front of the windows this summer," said Tilden. Dewey took a sip of tea. "It's a nice place to write, isn't it?

"And DePaul has a creative writing class that's less than a three-block walk from here."

"So, after the summer, then what? I wouldn't wait too long to start interviewing. You can cover up a small lapse in your resume, but if you wait too long—"

"My business career is over. Zach did me a favor."

Dewey set her cup down abruptly, splashing tea on the computer keypad. She wheeled in the chair to face him. "Both of you are so stubborn. He won't talk about it and you refuse to discuss it; I mean none of it makes any sense at all. I'm sure if you approached him, hat in hand—"

Tilden used his napkin to blot up the spilled tea. "I think the thing I hate most about business is the proliferation of the cliché."

"He's selling the station in Montgomery," said Dewey.

"But television is the engine of Lesser's future," said Tilden. "And you can quote me."

"For a sixty-five million dollar profit," said Dewey.

There it was again. That's all the justification she needed for anything. The money. The profit. She was the supreme capitalist. Like Zach. She was just like him. Tilden wanted her to see him for what he was, but all she saw was a man with a halo of dollar signs over his head.

Until that Saturday morning when Tilden spotted the first reference to Zach and Sonya in the *Tribune's* morning gossip column. Cookie Martin's column. *Which Northshore socialite is having trouble keeping her husband out of New York?* was the first mention. Then: *Will a face-lift and tummy tuck be enough for a certain publishing heiress to keep her hubby?* And: *Which buttery-blond mondaine (initials S.L.) just hired Chicago's most ferocious divorce attorney?* Day-by-day, week-by-week, the story unfolded. That Zach had a girlfriend in Manhattan seemed even to take Dewey by surprise. That the woman in question was none other than an employee of Barton, Endres, a girl twenty years younger than Zach, a girl who couldn't quite keep her acne under control due to an uninterrupted diet of corn crisps, potato chips, buttered popcorn and Pepsi Cola, a girl who brandished her Harvard degree like a pistol, a girl who had treated Tilden like an errand boy and Dewey like a secretary, a girl who now rode onto the scene to rescue Tilden from the suffocating stench of Zach's business conquests.

"What can he possibly see in that dyke?" said Dewey. "Her roots are an inch long before she notices and those slut-red fingernails are atrocious."

"It almost sounds like you're in love with him," said Tilden. "I mean, after all, he's married to Sonya." And without a response Dewey got up to take her shower.

Gradually, though, things were good again between them. Tenderness became a part of their lovemaking; Dewey laughed more easily and stopped complaining about Tilden's basement apartment and she called more frequently during the day too, even when she was out of town with Zach. Things were so good that the only time Dewey seemed angry was when Zach's girlfriend's name came up. *Trillia*. It might as well have been a synonym for *tsunami* or *tornado* or *typhoon*. Otherwise things were so good that Tilden and Dewey began to discuss the prospect of marriage.

They were having breakfast one Saturday morning at the pancake house on Clark Street. "You must never talk about anything I tell you about the office," said Dewey.

Who would he tell? None of his friends in the writing group cared a whit about business. None of them had even heard of Zach or Lesser Limited. None of them had anything good to say about any of Tilden's stories that dealt with business. They thought it was interesting that Tilden could afford to write all day without working as a bartender or waiter at night to support himself, but as to the actual mechanics or workings of business, as seen by a former insider, they couldn't care less. Tilden looked at Dewey and shook his head.

"Because the things that happen at Lesser are confidential," she said. "Zach needs me and he depends on me, but if he thought I discussed work outside the office he'd get rid of me. If he thought you and I were…you know we're taking a chance even being in this restaurant," she said, and then began to look around the room, her eyes darting here and there in rapid, abrupt bird-like movements.

And then, apparently assured that it was safe, she continued in conspiratorial tones, leaning over her stack of blueberry pancakes. Zach had a plan: he had a buyer for Suzie-Sox and another for the radio stations and was even in negotiations to sell Lesser Learning Systems. Zach was disbanding the company, selling it off, piece-by-piece, bit-by-bit. Lesser was becoming less and less, more and more limited every day. If the individual entities brought what it looked like they were going to bring in the liquidation, Barton, Endres stood to make more than a billion dollars profit and Zach himself might make as much two hundred million dollars. Oh, and yes, Dewey's shares were probably going to be worth at least five million. "So," she announced, leaning back in her chair and bending her head forward, "all we have to do is be patient until the corporation is liquidated and Lesser is no more and then we get married." She smiled and reached across the table and held his hand.

Now they had a secret to share. The basement apartment became their safe house. No danger of Zach stopping by unexpectedly with an important letter for Dewey to type; no danger of Zach calling at 6 A.M. to dictate a memorandum; no danger of Zach driving by and seeing them enter or leave her apartment. As long as Dewey checked her messages and returned his calls, there was no danger from Zach at all. Truth was, Tilden knew, Zach was too preoccupied with Trillia to bother Dewey unless it was absolutely necessary. Dewey occasionally went into convulsive rages when she came back from a New York trip, and the subject of these rages was always Trillia. How she came into every meeting carrying a can of Pepsi and a bag of greasy chips, how she had festering, puss-filled open sores on her face, how she had the audacity to change Zach's lunch order one day at Smith and Wollensky's steakhouse insisting that he have fish or chicken and not a sirloin, how she reached over right during a meeting and caressed his arm with those blood-colored nails of hers. Tilden remembered her and had to agree; he couldn't quite imagine the attraction—maybe Trillia dressed up as a cheerleader or a bobby-soxer car hop and they made love in the back of Zach's limousine—but he didn't really care. With Zach out of the picture, life was sweet.

Tilden sat at his desk stumbling through a first draft. At times he believed that business had ruined any chance he had of writing decent fiction. His first drafts were strewn with clichés, and after years of writing analytical reports and memoranda he struggled to subvert the urge to make sense, the drive to be clear and logical. Overwriting, explaining, using clichés—these tendencies were: *nails in the coffin, straws that broke the camel's back, kisses of death,* for his prose.

He looked up and was staring out his window at the blooming tulips when he saw a red Falcon convertible drive by: a car which looked at first glance like his mothers, with the top down, though it was spring and the air still chilled. The driver wore a dark, heavy coat and some sort of tight-fitted cap pulled down over his ears. A red scarf, fastened at his neck, billowed in his wake. Tilden stood, leaned forward and looked through the window to the south. The Falcon had pulled in the neighbor's driveway and was backing out. Tilden watched as the car parked on the street right in front of him; he watched as the driver got out of the car and looked first at his apartment windows and then toward the side entrance of the building; he watched as the fellow, in knee-high, brown boots and matching bomber jacket, unsnapped his flapped, leather helmet and removed the snug-fitting goggles.

Tilden jumped up, ran to the side door, and unlocked it.

"I'm so happy for you two that I had to come up and tell you in person," said his mother, as she threw her arms around him. "Dewey called me yesterday morning; she couldn't keep the secret any longer."

Tilden pulled his mother into the room and closed the door. At first he was relieved (Dewey wasn't pregnant) and then miffed (What right did Dewey have to reveal their wedding plans without consulting him?) and finally he was irate (Dewey told his mother that she wanted to be married in a vintage, Ford Trimotor airplane while they flew over Lake Michigan). She wanted to turn their marriage into a circus, something that might receive mention on one of those sleazy, TV magazine shows.

And the absurd thing was, Tilden's mother had been all for it. Just like she had supported Dewey's idea for the honeymoon and not his.

Dewey fidgeted during the entire performance and said very little during the intermissions, except to express her opinion that the woman singing the role of Mimi was pretty fat, but Tilden managed to stay relaxed and upbeat until after the final curtain call when they stood outside the Opera House in the brittle cold. It was an anniversary of sorts: four years since they met outside the glass windows of Lesser's conference room.

It wasn't a great performance, Tilden knew, but there were moments. Still, his aesthetic disappointment had no doubt sparked his anger. Taxis were flagged the instant they appeared on the street; the temperature, according to the digital sign atop the office tower on the other side of Wacker Drive, read minus twenty, and the wind blew with relentless force, spinning through the high-rise buildings like an Arctic dervish.

"I have an alternate suggestion for our honeymoon," said Dewey.

"Instead of Europe?" And he thought she meant South America or Asia or Australia. "But what about Paris? What about Amsterdam? Don't you want to hear the Concertgebouw? You'd love the Rijksmuseum," said Tilden.

Dewey's shoulders shook in the cold; she pulled her muffler up over her nose and mouth. Her breath crystallized, penetrating the wool scarf, escaping into the air as she said, "I've got brochures." Ice formed on the muffler outlining the shape of her mouth. "Let's go on a rock climbing trip. Out West. Wouldn't you rather be outside and not cooped up in some stuffy museum?"

That night she wanted to make love. Tilden lay with his back to her. He looked out across the basement, past the area which served as a living room, to his desk and computer in the space below the front windows. He felt Dewey's fingernails on the back of his neck, his shoulders, down his backbone. She reached over and took his penis in her hand. Tilden clenched his teeth, stifled his breathing, and after a minute or so, she let go and turned over.

❧•❧

Dewey stands on one side of the bed, and Tilden stands on the other. He turns away and walks to the window. The woman in the room of the Ambassador West directly across, the one he saw earlier in the evening, is back too. Framed by the light from behind, she removes her earrings, sets them down on a dresser and then looks up. For a moment she appears to focus on him; something in her bearing makes Tilden believe that she is alone. After she pulls the draperies closed, he closes his as well.

When he turns around, Dewey has removed all her clothing except for her slip. She gets into bed, pulls the sheet up to her waist. Tilden steps out of his shoes, unbuckles his trousers and takes off his shirt. He sits on the edge of the bed to remove his socks. Not looking at her, he says, "Are you sure?"

When she doesn't respond right away, he turns his head and looks at her. She nods. It isn't a pronounced or sweeping movement—her head is sunk into the pillow and that restricts her range of motion—but she does nod. Tilden might interpret this as a lack of commitment on her part, but when she smiles faintly and puts her hand up to her mouth, he realizes that she is anxious. Surprised, he lies beside her, turns onto his hip and puts his arm over her; she turns onto her hip now too, so that she faces him; slowly he moves closer and she raises her head off the pillow and they kiss: a long, lazy kiss, full of tenderness and memories, but one which lacks passion.

When Tilden comes out of the bathroom in the morning, he smells coffee and bacon. Dewey has called room service: a table has been set up next to the window. She removes the stainless steel covers and holds them like cymbals. "Scrambled eggs, bacon—you still eat bacon I hope—and rye toast." Seeing her in her uniform again, and standing next to the table, makes her look more like a ship's steward than a pilot, and Tilden has to suppress a smile. She puts down the cymbals, sits at the table, and spreads the linen napkin across her lap. When she looks up at him, Tilden comes over to the table and sits down too.

"You didn't sleep very well last night, did you?" he says.

"Do I look that bad?"

He awoke several times during the night, and each time Dewey had gotten up and was in the bathroom, except for the last time, at 4 A.M. when she sat in the chair close to the foot of the bed. She sat, staring, a shadow in the semidarkness, and he pretended that he was still asleep to watch her through squinted eyes. They had always slept so well together, nestling like spoons, turning in unison, often sharing the same pillow, but that was so long ago and she'd been sleeping with a husband he didn't even know while he'd been sleeping alone. Had he thought they'd fit together again, easily, like two lost pieces in a jigsaw puzzle? How naive. How foolish.

"About last night," says Tilden. "I'm sorry. I thought—"

"Come on, Tilden. You would never have stayed if I hadn't engineered it. I know you so well. It's so important for you to please people. It's one of the qualities that I love about you. Face it, I manipulated you again." Her tone is soft, her voice sad.

She has few regrets in life, she says, and seeing Tilden has given her a chance to apologize for her most grievous. Everything she has done in life seems an attempt to escape the earth and its boundaries, while Tilden understands that to escape the earth is to leave people and their creations behind. People are Tilden's reason for existing. She says all this, and though he knows she has overstated the degree of his contentment, he does not object.

"Have you ever heard of Fibro Myalgia Syndrome?" she says.

He shakes his head.

"The doctors believe I have it."

Tilden finishes chewing his mouthful of toast and bacon, swallows, and wipes his mouth with his napkin. There are whole generations of illnesses and maladies that he realizes he knows little or nothing of: lethal viruses escaping from the rain forest, bacteria in the earth that make people suffer flu-like symptoms, poisonous gases seeping from the ground through concrete into people's homes, fungi growing in peoples' bodies that were unheard of until the discovery and use of antibiotics. The prefix fibro makes him think of growth-gone-wrong: tumors—and yes, cancer.

"I'll have to quit flying," she says. She cocks her head, as if waiting for his response. Tilden takes a sip of coffee, but resists the urge to ask questions or fill the void with words. Instead, he keeps looking at her until she continues. And eventually, she does. "In some ways the worst is over," she says. "The average time to diagnose FMS is three years." Then she catalogues the symptoms: muscle twitching, stiffness and pain, fatigue, lack of deep, stage-four sleep, soreness in the joints, occasional mental confusion. "Many of them are the same as Lupus and Multiple Sclerosis," she says. "For a long time they thought I might have Lou Gehrig's Disease."

"But you don't? Right? And this Fibro—"

"FMS—"

"Isn't fatal?"

She shakes her head. With luck, she tells him, it might play itself out in three to five years, if she can reduce the level of stress in her life.

Tilden rubs his face and eyes, vigorously, to stimulate the circulation. He looks at her and squints. "Now, what airlines did you say you fly for again?"

Dewey smiles. "That's not funny, Tilden. In fact it's a little cruel." She deposits her napkin on the table and stands up. She retrieves her purse and takes out a compact. "I'm taking a leave of absence. This is my last day."

Dewey sits at the foot of the bed, next to Tilden's chair, and examines her face in her compact. "For months I was convinced I was going to die. The thought of leaving Daisy without a mother—" Dewey puts her hand on her forehead. Tilden watches as a tear wells in the corner of her eye; when it starts down alongside her nose, he reaches over and puts his hand on her knee. "I've thought about you so often, Tilden" she says, pushing the tear away with her index finger. She takes a tissue from her purse and wipes her nose. "At the time, I wanted to tell you about the low-ball appraisal."

"I knew what the liquidation would bring."

"Of course you always said you suspected—"

"I knew." He just never allowed himself to think that Dewey knew—about the appraisal. The idea of the two of them in cahoots against him was something that he had steadfastly refused to consider. Despite Sonya.

⁊•⁊

Sonya took two steps back from her husband's desk. She removed the wool cap, shook her hair loose. Tilden had never seen her hair look better; it actually fell, it actually moved, it actually resembled something other than what one would see on a mannequin. And she wore no makeup. She began slowly to un-button her raincoat. She let it drop to the floor then pulled off her sweater. She wore no bra either, and her breasts—surgically-enhanced he realized now—were as large and swollen and rigid as mercury-filled rubber. She reached to her hip, unzipped her skirt. It fell to the floor; Sonya stepped out of it, and still wearing the spiked black boots, took his hand and led him to the blue sofa that sat along the south-facing wall. She moved to the doorway and turned off the lights, and Tilden peered at the sofa, illuminated by intermittent flashes of lightning. He visualized Zach: sitting at one end, feet barely touching the floor, with pa-pers spread out around him on the plush, velvet cushions. Sonya returned, pushed Tilden onto those cushions and straddled his chest. Reaching behind, she unzipped his fly and touched his penis. Without all the mascara and powder and hair spray and glossy lipstick, Sonya was a rather pretty woman, and Tilden felt the surge of an erection.

"Well," said Sonya. "Lucky Dewey." She slid back until she sat on his ankles. Then she unfastened his belt and slid his pants down over his hips and jerked down his shorts. Tilden flinched: there was something of the dominatrix in her manner as she took him firmly in her right hand and squeezed. "And lucky Sonya," she said, as she bent to take him in her mouth.

❧•❧

"Remember the blue sofa in Zach's office?" says Tilden.

"The one you said looked like a coffin," says Dewey. "Sure. Why?"

Dewey's eyes are dry now, but the eyelids and surrounding skin are sulfated and red. Perhaps he simply knows what to look for now, but there are so many signs of erosion on her face: small rivers at the corners of the mouth, streams that form deltas at the edges of the eyes, canyons etched into her forehead. But so what if her face has been lined by stress, so what if facts about her health have caused the flesh along her jaw line to sag, so what if her cheeks are no longer as firm or toned. These changes prove that she is ephemeral and vulnerable; these changes are part of her history. But it's a history which he hasn't shared.

"Did you ever notice that when Zach sat on it, his feet didn't touch the floor?" says Tilden.

The sky is gray and sunless when they climb into the cab. There are no actual, visible clouds; it is just typical Chicago weather: overcast, dull, and foggy. But Tilden doesn't complain, and neither does Dewey. They hold hands as the driver merges onto the expressway at Ontario. Tilden looks into the rear view mirror, but the man's eyes don't look back; he is apparently not interested in his passengers. The taxi keeps to the left, enters the express lanes to O'Hare.

After his father left, his mother did not heat the entire house. He remembers now the nightly ritual of warming his pillow on the space heater in the center room. He thinks of his bed, wedged in the corner against the wall, and hears the rain outside the window. Whenever he sees that room he remembers the game of undressing that he played on rainy winter nights; there was something about the sound of water drumming on the window sill that made him happy and sad at the same time. He stepped across the bare wood floor to place the pillow and blankets and his pajamas on the chair, then he lay on his back without clothes in the middle of the bed on the cold sheets. He lay like that, sometimes for half an hour and sometimes longer, ignoring the chill, until at last he allowed himself to acquire— one by one—the lost items. First the pajama bottoms, then the top, then the pillow, then the top thin sheet, then the light wool blanket, and finally, the top heavy quilt.

As an adult, Tilden thinks there are many layers of meaning to that childhood game, and though it does not rain often where he lives now, he is able sometimes at night to imagine himself as an old man, naked and alone in a small, cold bed, with rain beating a tattoo on his bedroom window.

Dewey, who has been resting her head on his shoulder, suddenly sits straight. "Zach was so jealous of you," she says.

"Right," says Tilden.

"Really," she says.

༺ • ༻

Zach placed his feet precisely and addressed the ball deliberately, bringing the head of the club to within a half inch of the dimpled surface, before withdrawing to repeat the process. He had played each hole as carefully as if this were the Masters' Tournament with Tilden and him tied in the final round. It wasn't until late in the day, after they had played nine holes, that Zach spoke for the first time.

"Til, did you ever wonder why my father-in-law and I have the same name? Did you think it was simply an idle coincidence?"

"Well, yes, I suppose I did," said Tilden.

Zach worked the plunger of the ball cleaner up and down, withdrew the ball, and held it at eye level to examine it. "When I married Sonya, I saw an opportunity. I respect a man who knows an opportunity when he sees one, Tilden."

Tilden sat on the bench and watched as Zach inserted another ball in the cleaning apparatus.

"I had my name legally changed to Zachary. Needless to say, the old man was quite moved." Zach sat down next to Tilden, crossed his legs at the knee, and leaned back. He reached in the pocket of his lemon-yellow trousers and took out a nail clipper. He opened out the flat-edged cleaning tool and began to scrape under his nails, though Tilden noticed that he reaped very little, if any, foreign matter. Zach worked silently—first the right hand and then the left—taking special care with the thumbs, as if by simply trimming, filing, and pushing back the skin around the cuticles he could distract people from the foreshortened distal phalanges.

"You see, when I changed my name, Tilden, I created a positive opportunity." Zach folded up the nail clipper and slipped it back in his pocket.

Tilden had been looking out over the golf course. The fairways were lush, the greens in magnificent shape, even the rough areas surrounding the course had a manicured look about them. Zach had always sought out, had always enjoyed the best of everything. The best country club, the best suburb, the best yacht club. What was next? A string of polo ponies?

Tilden looked over at Zach and saw that he was staring at him, his angry jaw set forward, the muscle in his cheek tensed and flexing. He obviously wished to extract an apology from Tilden. Did he expect him to roll over and expose his crotch like some cowering, mangy dog?

A meadowlark sang from a branch of a cottonwood, and a monarch butterfly fluttered in the sunshine just out of reach. Tilden looked at Zach. "Do you think the size of a man's penis matters to women, Zach? As much as it matters to men, I mean. Do you think they talk about how well-endowed we are behind our backs? Do you think they compare notes?"

And at the junction in terminal number two, where Concourse A joins Concourse B, where Tilden first saw Dewey gliding round the corner, they embrace. Tilden kisses Dewey's neck; the guava-scented fragrance of her cologne fills his nostrils. They hug, pat, sway left and right, then finally release their hold on one another and step apart. Dewey straightens her posture, puts on her cap, pulls it down tight.

"Tilden," she says.

"Yes."

"In your stories…"

"Yes."

"Do you ever write about me?"

"Sometimes."

"Send me one," she says.

Tilden nods.

She angles her head, down and to the right, and looks at him as if she knows he has a question. "What?" she says.

"Nothing," he says.

"Tilden, what is it?"

"Does Brad have dysplastic distal phalanges?" he says.

She laughs. "Tilden, you're an idiot."

"Is he tall?"

"He's about your height," she says. "Why?"

"Just curious," he says.

She smiles at him for a moment, and then shakes her head as if suddenly nonplussed. She puts her hand to his cheek before reaching to pick up her case. Then she turns and starts to walk away. She only takes three or four steps before she turns around again. "Tilden?"

"Yes."

"I'll bet your stories are funny."

Tilden smiles and watches as Dewey walks away. He watches as she makes her way down the corridor, head held high above those around her. He is halfway down his own concourse, halfway to his own gate, when he turns around and runs back. He takes a seat in the lounge by the plate glass window. A seat where he can see the silhouette of Dewey's head through the airplane windshield. He watches as she checks gauges and flips switches; he watches when she backs away from the jet way, away from the terminal; he watches as she turns and taxies out to the runway. Then he walks to the end of the terminal, and with his nose pressed against the glass like a child waving goodbye to his grandparents, he watches her speed past on the runway. The engines scream, and the glass rattles and the jet's nose angles up sharply. The wheels leave the ground and the plane climbs, swift and steep. Just before it reaches the ceiling of cloud cover, there is a minute opening in the leaden sky, not a glare of light, not enough to make Tilden shade his eyes, but enough to reflect off the red insignia on the plane's tail, enough to bathe the yellow wings and the orange fuselage in one, long, golden shaft of sunshine.

A Romanze
For Martha

I. OVERTURE

THE BELL ABOVE THE DOOR of Martha's shop jingled, and she looked up from her journal of inventory items. The customer chose a path up a narrow aisle, stepping around the chairs and tables and bookcases that filled the room until he stood beside the roll top desk where Martha sat working. The man's florid, unlined face suggested someone in his early- or mid-fifties, but the style and cut of his clothing made him appear older. And more conservative—a throwback in fact to an earlier era. In Madras blazer, cotton twill trousers, silk tie and straw fedora, one might expect such a man to be browsing the galleries east of Michigan Avenue and not the simpler stores that lined both sides of Clark Street in this uptown area of Chicago. He removed his hat and held it against his chest. "I'm looking for glass," he said, smiling. "Steuben, Lalique, Depression glass, ruby glass. Any glass, all glass—if it's pretty."

Martha considered his thinning brown hair, cut short as a concession to the receding hairline no doubt, then stood up from behind her desk and surveyed the room. She continued her inspection for a prolonged period before glancing down to consult her inventory ledger on the desktop. She thumbed the pages forward and backward and looked at the man again, who had stood patiently through all this with his hat in hand.

"I don't have much in the way of exceptional glass right now," Martha said. "If you're interested in porcelain or ceramics, I have some Wedgwood and Royal Doulton pieces."

"Your shop is charming, really charming," said the man. "I've been living in England for the last few years and this is the first time I've been into the city since I returned." He looked around the store. "Just as quaint as can be. Is that Vivaldi I hear? This is really so much more typical of the shops in London than Chicago. Forgive me; I'm Nash Winters," he said, bowing. "It is your shop, isn't it? It's lovely in any event."

Martha offered her hand and nodded. "Martha Simmons," she said. "England. Well. Let me think. Pretty glass. You must have had access to all kinds of Wedgwood and Royal Doulton, living in London," she said. The frames of the man's glasses were light-weight and thin, probably alloyed metal, but the lenses themselves were dark and tinted against glare, which made it possible for Martha to see the wall behind her and her own re-flection but not Mr. Nash Winters' eyes. She smiled. "Yes, it is my shop—and thank you." Nash Winters set his fedora on a bare spot on the topmost portion of the roll top and took an engraved silver-plate cigarette case from his inside jacket pocket.

"Do you mind if I smoke?" he said.

Martha hesitated. "Actually," she said, "with the books and all—"

"Certainly, I concede it's a filthy habit, but I'm afraid after England…they're a few years back in terms of no-smoking regu-lations, you know," said Nash Winters, apparently unfazed, though any reading of his countenance through the murky lenses of his *spectacles* was quite impossible. He closed the cigarette case and returned it to his breast pocket. "I found a remarkable com-memorative plate once, just over the Scottish border in a town called Jedborough, made of Doulton and numbered. It had this lovely green and plum-colored drawing of Victoria and Albert on the occasion of their wedding in 1840. When I got back to Lon-don, my friend broke it. Shattered it into a hundred miniscule fragments in the lavatory. *An accident*, he said. Whatever. I don't think I ever mourned a broken object more. It had lacey gold edging and the most absurd cartoon-like rendering of Albert in full military garb—and then there was poor chinless Victoria staring at him with adoring eyes."

Martha nodded periodically till certain that Nash Winters was finished with his story. A talkative fellow for sure, though she enjoyed the opportunity to not be responsible for carrying a conversation—or making a sales pitch for that matter. "Victoriana," she said. "I have something you might like." She fished her shoes out from under the desk, one at a time with her right foot, so as not to draw attention to the fact that she'd been barefoot while she worked. After she'd stepped back into her shoes, she took a ring of keys from one of the roll top drawers, pulled her blouse down over her hips and moved out and away from the desk. "It's over there, in the china cabinet with the glass doors, against the wall," she said, pointing.

Martha held the edges of her full cotton skirt as she negotiated her way among the pieces of furniture so as not to knock over any small items. Damage was enough of a problem from customers in these cramped quarters without a contribution from her in unnecessary haste. In front of the cabinet, she examined her key ring until she located the L-shaped, rusted one, unlike any of the other keys. "It's the raw umber and burnt sienna pitcher commemorating the Golden Jubilee in 1887—on the top shelf," she said, inserting the key. "It's Doulton."

"But what's that under it on the middle shelf?"

Martha swung the glass doors open, first the right and then the left. "The tea service?" she said.

"The colors are fabulous," said Nash Winters.

"It's circa World War I," said Martha, wondering how he could appreciate color through his shaded lenses. "From what was then called Czecho-Slovakia," she said. She took the teapot from its place on the glass shelf and held it out to him. "I don't know if it's rare or not. I suppose I should, being in the business and all. Be careful; it's so thin it's almost translucent." Nash Winters held the teapot in his left palm and ran the index finger of his right hand on the lid's surface and, as he conducted his examination, he whistled through his teeth. Martha watched him for a moment then reached in to get the creamer.

She turned it over and showed Nash Winters the imprint and crest on the bottom. "See how the spelling is hyphenated; that shows it's from the end of The Great War. After that, they spelled it as one word and dropped the hyphenation. Now of course it's two separate republics."

"You're a history buff," said Nash Winters.

Martha averted her eyes, took a deep breath and said, "I'm not a date and statistic aficionado, if that's what you mean—though I do enjoy the personal details that bring history to life."

Nash Winters frowned and nodded, indicating that he understood. Then he unbuttoned his sport coat and thrust his hands into the pockets of his trousers. Leaning forward and inclining his head toward Martha, he said, "I agree with you about the dates. But what kind of personal details? Give me an example of something that brings history alive for you?"

Over Nash Winters' left shoulder on the Biedermeier dining table near the front display window, sat the silver-plate samovar Martha had acquired at the yard sale in the old Estonian neighborhood near the Loop. "Well," she began, "for example, did you know that when the Czar and his family were murdered the princesses had so many jewels hidden inside their long dresses that the bullets mostly ricocheted off of them? The executioners had to plunge the bayonets of their rifles into the girls repeatedly to actually kill them. Imagine what that must have been like for those innocent girls."

The customer's red face darkened and he leaned back. Other than the heightened ruddiness though, Nash Winters showed no visible reaction, nor did he comment. After a while, perhaps to fill the void because Martha didn't amplify her remarks or make any further comment either, he laughed. Not nervous laughter, but raucous from-the-belly glee, suggesting that either he didn't believe her story or, worse, that he did and found it humorous. Nash Winters laughed so long and so hard that perspiration began to appear on his forehead and he started to cough and then, Martha presumed, because his eyes had begun to water, the man finally removed the cherished glasses. Still convulsing, he folded them and held them in his left hand. Martha couldn't determine the color of his irises while he laughed, but the crinkling around his eyes suggested a good-hearted man who laughed frequently and enjoyed life to the fullest extent. His joy was infectious to be sure, and Martha put her hand to her mouth and chuckled.

When Nash Winters finished laughing and coughing and crying, he took a handkerchief from his hip pocket and mopped his face and blew his nose. Afterward he put the handkerchief back and said, "I need a drink. I could really use a drink. It's almost five. Could I buy you a cocktail?"

"Your eyes are green," said Martha. Then, realizing what Nash Winters had just said, she looked away. Since the man had been in her store for twenty minutes at most, the invitation came as a surprise, and she felt her face coloring. "I'm in the middle of inventory and there isn't anyone to watch the shop."

"Can't twist your arm?"

"Thank you," she said, "but no." She turned away and closed the glass doors of the cabinet and started to lock them again. She cleared her throat. "If you're hungry there's a lovely place—"

"I'll take the tea set," said Nash Winters. "The Czecho-Slovakian tea set. How much is it?"

"Oh," said Martha. She pulled the doors back open and dropped her hands to dry her perspiring palms on her skirt. "Of course. The tea set. I have a bit invested in it," she said. "I'm asking a thousand, but—"

"Fine. You'll accept cash?" said Winters. He winked and waited as if for confirmation, and Martha nodded in silence.

"I'll get a box and some bubble wrap," she said, suddenly feeling that she needed to take action—any kind of action—to control the direction of events. Nash Winters wasn't exactly her idea of a sex symbol, but something about him made her feel susceptible; she smiled and stifled a yawn in an effort to make this seem like just another business transaction.

Still holding his glasses, Nash Winters placed his other hand on her shoulder and patted. "Don't bother with that now," he said. "You're busy with your inventory. I'll pay and send someone to pick it up later." He put his glasses on again, nudging them into place at the bridge with his thumb, then reached into the breast pocket of his jacket and extracted a long, slender wallet resembling a checkbook. He counted out ten shiny, unwrinkled one-hundred-dollar bills—the redesigned bills with the enlarged, off-center portrait of Benjamin Franklin on the front—and thrust the cash at Martha without ceremony. She couldn't help but notice that there were still a great many crisp-looking notes left in the billfold. "You have beautiful hair," Nash Winters said, "and gorgeous complexion."

Martha opened her mouth then closed it to swallow. "Thank you, again," she said at last. "Let me get you a receipt." She turned, hurried over to the roll top and searched in the clutter for her receipt book. "I must get a computer," she said. "When would you like to pick up the tea service?" Nash Winters stood with his back to her, still peering into the china cabinet. "Excuse me, Mr. Winters," said Martha, "when would you like to pick up the merchandize?"

He turned. "*Nash*, please. Call me *Nash*." He made his way back, a different route this time, and stood next to her at the desk. He took his hat from the spot where he had left it and put it on. "How about Saturday afternoon? My assistant will be in town picking up some other things, and I could get him to—

"Wait a sec. I've got an idea…I apologize, what was your name again?"

"Martha Simmons," said Martha. She couldn't be certain because Nash Winters had put his glasses back on, but he may have glanced down to look at her hands.

"Well, Miss Martha Simmons," he said, "it is *Miss*, isn't it?" Martha nodded and attempted to smile, but her cheeks simply jerked as if afflicted by a nervous twitch. "You might enjoy seeing my glassware collection," said Nash Winters. "Why don't you come out to the farm for supper?"

Martha sat down and rested her elbows on the arms of her chair. She shook her head. "You don't have to do that," she said.

"Alain can bring you out with the tea set, and I'll have him drive you back after supper. I don't know what time you close, but if six isn't too early it'll still be light and you can see the horses. I'm in Darlington Hills. Did I say?" Before Martha could respond, Winters pressed on. "Should Alain come here or would you prefer for him to pick you up at home?"

"I live here," said Martha. She pointed to the ceiling, and Nash Winters puckered his mouth. "Upstairs," she said. "Over my shop."

"Oh my, that is quaint," said Nash Winters. "You are so lucky, Martha. Please don't tell me that you have another engagement Saturday night."

ℭℬ II. SCHERZO

FOR THE SECOND TIME since she bought the building and opened the store, a year ago now, Martha closed early. Upstairs she inserted the Concerto in D Minor, by Antonio Vivaldi, in the CD player (Nash Winters had commented on the Vivaldi when he came into the shop on Tuesday) and then she stood to look out the front window of her greystone two-flat. The traffic situation worsened week by week; there was almost never metered parking available on Clark Street now that summer had arrived. Traffic was good for business, for sure, but if people couldn't get out of their cars, what difference did it make? She herself would only circle a block a few times before giving up.

The hard rain that had fallen throughout the day lessened, though the drizzle persisted. Couples and groups were lined up across the street, waiting for the Creperie to open, but this Saturday she wouldn't be there, eating alone at the small table under the stairwell and next to the coat rack. The owners, a sweet couple from Brittany, greeted her like a treasured friend each time she came in and, with a great deal of fanfare, proclaimed: "Mademoiselle, your usual table is prepared."

Martha walked through her dining room, touched the package containing the Czecho-Slovakian tea service, wrapped in green and brown gift paper with the repeating design of grazing horses and tied up with yellow ribbon, then went on into the bedroom to take out the dress she planned to wear.

Yesterday evening (the first time she had ever closed the store early) Martha had taken the train down to Marshall Fields'. She picked out a black, mid-length linen dress then took the elevator to the fifth floor to get a new pair of shoes. Seeing the box now on the carpet at the foot of the bed, made her mouth dry; she reached into the pocket of her dress and took out a butterscotch. She put the candy in her mouth, sat on the edge of the bed and picked up the box containing the new footwear. She took off the lid, folded the tissue over the edges and removed one of the shoes. The thick platform soles were all right (she could use a little more height); it was the leopard-print straps, with the one encircling the toe that made her mouth dry. And the silver daisy on top, designed to look like a toe ring…But the salesgirl with the hennaed hair and pierced nose had insisted, "These shoes are so cool for you."

For the first few days after Nash Winters purchased the tea set, Martha refused to take his invitation seriously. She knew nothing about the man, really, except for the fact that he collected glass; for all she could tell he might be a serial murderer who bound and gagged his victims and sang opera while slashing them with a polished dueling saber. The world was a bloody place—that much she did know—and so after several days of reflection, she had decided that if Nash Winters did telephone to renew his request she would politely decline. Then she saw his picture on the front page of the "Metro" section of the *Chicago Tribune*. The Benevolent Brotherhood of something or other had named him *Person of the Decade* for his *unflagging dedication and tireless efforts to reverse the blight of inner-city neighborhoods.* According to the accompanying article, his most recent contribution would enable the organization to build a much-needed recreation center in a seedy area southwest of the Loop. So much for Nash Winters' credentials.

And then in the gift store up the street, when she was purchasing wrapping paper, Martha mentioned her customer—and the fact that he had horses—to the elderly woman who waited on her. The woman, who bore a striking resemblance to Eleanor Roosevelt, had looked at Martha as if she had just claimed to have never heard of Mother Teresa. "The Winters are a very prominent industrial family," the woman said, shaking her large head. "Big political contributors too."

All this knowledge had initially reassured Martha, and when Nash Winters' assistant called to relay the expected time of his arrival the coming Saturday evening she had assured the fellow that she would be ready. Now, however, as the appointed hour drew near, she began to pace the room.

But even though she could refuse to accompany Nash Winters' assistant back to Darlington (she could say she wasn't feeling well; it wouldn't be much of an exaggeration) she still showered, put on the linen dress and leopard-strapped shoes and stood in front of the mirrored closet doors to apply lipstick. The new clothes made her hairstyle look dated and the black linen material enabled her to see something that she hadn't previously noticed: several strands of gray at the beginning of her scalp above her forehead. Too many to pluck out, so she took her purse from the top of the dresser, collected the wrapped tea service in the dining room and went downstairs to wait for Nash Winters' assistant.

In the shop, Martha unlocked the jewelry case and took out the tortoise-shell hairclips then chose the dangling turquoise earrings and matching necklace. She put on the earrings, fastened the necklace and was adjusting the hairclips when she saw the young man in the outside alcove of the doorway. If this was indeed the assistant, in black T-shirt and blue jeans, he was thirty minutes early.

She unfastened the deadbolt and opened the door. "Are you here for Mr. Winters' parcel?" said Martha.

"*Sí, sí*," said the man, "I am Alain St. Germain."

Martha introduced herself. "You're early," she said. "Come in for moment out of the weather and I'll get my things."

Alain St. Germain stepped across the threshold, but no further. Framed in the doorway, he glanced around the room and said, "Where is the package? I must put the package in the Daimler."

"Please?" said Martha.

Alain St. Germain inhaled a breath. "I must put Nash's package in the car with the others and wait for you. Where is the package?"

Martha pointed to the Chippendale sideboard, not two feet from where he stood. "With the yellow ribbon. No need to wait. I'm ready," said Martha. "I'll get my umbrella."

On the sidewalk, she locked the door to her shop and turned to see the black limousine in the street with its emergency lights flashing. Though it had been pulled close to the parked cars at the meters, the vehicle contributed to the slowing of traffic, already hobbled by rain in the narrow thoroughfare. Apparently oblivious to the honking horns and the cursing of at least one driver through his open window, Alain St. Germain stood in the inclement weather, holding open the back door. Though the rain had intensified again, Martha didn't undo her umbrella, choosing instead to dash the short distance to the car.

Alain St. Germain closed the door after Martha sat inside and went around the back of the automobile to open the driver's door and get in behind the wheel. He maneuvered the grand car into southbound traffic and turned west onto Irving Park Road.

Traffic was less snarled in this direction, but neither Alain St. Germain nor Martha attempted conversation. She studied the cavernous interior of the limousine with its cracked-leather upholstery and folded jump seats. The assistant had curly black hair and a pronounced accent, and she judged him to be younger than Winters, no more than twenty-five or thirty at most. And he was taller too.

After half an hour, the young man pulled onto the Kennedy Expressway. Traffic here moved at a steady pace, notwithstanding the rain pelting on the roof and the spray washing over the road's surface. "This is a lovely old car," said Martha, in a loud voice. "What kind did you say?"

"A Daimler. This is the same the Queen drives. Nash have it shipped from England." Alain St. Germain looked at her in the rearview mirror.

"And where are you from, may I ask? Do I detect a Spanish accent?" said Martha.

The young man averted his eyes from the mirror. "I am from Argentina. In Argentina we speak the purest *Espanish*." And that was it for conversation until nearly an hour later, after they had left the expressway, driven through Darlington, and proceeded northwest on a rolling, curved country road. "Fifteen minutes," said Alain St. Germain. Martha looked at her watch, wiped the condensation off of her window with a tissue, and peered into the mist. True to his word, in fifteen minutes the driver slowed, braked harder and prepared to turn in between stone pillars. "Welcome to Rabbit Run Farms," he said.

The drive was lined with poplars and white fences—beyond that she couldn't see much in the rain—but after a few minutes they drove past a cluster of white barns and, a few yards further on, a road branching off to the right. They didn't take that road, but as they passed, the precipitation eased and the sky brightened, allowing Martha to see a columned white house on a rise in the distance and, next to the house in the clearing, the outline of what could only be a helicopter.

"That is the house of Nash's father," said Alain St. Germain.

"What business is he—Mr. Winters—in?" said Martha.

Mr. Winters is the very important business man," said Alain St. Germain. "His company is doing the most equipment of construction of the highways. Are you not of Chicago? Nash is but the modest one on his family."

"I only moved to Chicago a year ago, from Cincinnati," said Martha.

"And where is this *Cincinnati*? In America, yes?"

They drove along the banks of a lake where geese and ducks nested on the ground under two immense willows. And then they were out in the open again by more pastures, though Martha saw no horses.

Alain St. Germain turned his head suddenly toward Martha and spoke in a loud voice, surprising her. "Nash has the best beautiful parties. Mr. Winters' parties are for the boring people: the lawyers and the doctors and the *politicos*. At the Nash parties the guests ride on camels and wagons for hay. In the time of Christmas and snow we have strolls in the sleigh of the woods so they sing carols. The last month we have balloons of hot air for the people. You can see the horses—the most gorgeous racehorses—in the fields and over the farm. Nash has very amusing people. The artists, the actors, the writers, sports celebrities, television personalities, *modelos*."

"I'm excited about seeing his glassware. It must be quite wonderful," said Martha.

Alain St. Germain shrugged his shoulders. "Nash collects many things," he said.

The rain stopped completely as they turned onto a gravel driveway and approached a house, a chateau really, made of stone with a slate gambrel roof and an attached three-storey circular tower on one side. Alain St. Germain brought the car to a stop at the front of the house, but before he could get out, Martha's door was opened and there stood Nash Winters in a striped, long-sleeved polo shirt and jeans, a drink in hand, and even though the sun hadn't broken through, wearing sunglasses.

"What timing," he said. "Right as the rain stopped. Is it still coming down in the city?" Martha slid out of the seat, and Nash Winters stepped forward and kissed her on the cheek. "I'm terrifically pleased that you made it out. Can I get you a drink or shall we take a tour of the grounds while Alain unloads the car?"

Alain St. Germain glared at Nash Winters and then opened the trunk of the limousine without comment. When he leaned over to lift a parcel out of the filled trunk (not the gift-wrapped parcel from Martha's shop however), she noticed for the first time the width of his shoulders and the size of his arms.

"This was once an old stone barn, built a decade or so before the Civil War," said Nash Winters, "The most impressive feature of the place, I think, is the concrete silo here at the western end of the house." He took Martha's arm with his left hand and led her down the cobblestone walkway. Her foot slid sideways in her strapped shoe when she stepped on an uneven section of the path, and Nash Winters looked down at her feet. "My, what campy sandals," he said.

He gulped his drink and pointed to the top of the silo. A prominent feature of the circular roof, sloping up to a pinnacle and crowned with a weather vane, was a dormered foot-high birdhouse, which projected vertically from the slate surface. "I had to evict the bats before I could coax the orioles and wrens to move in. Wait till you see what I did on the inside of the silo. It has a circular staircase and an observatory at the top."

Martha followed as Nash Winters strode ahead on the rock path, around the silo to the back of the residence. Impatiens and marigolds edged the walkway, and at the base of the house were beds of flowering shrubs and dwarf trees, which she didn't recognize, but her host moved too quickly for her to inquire about them. In back, the lawn pitched up to a berm and stone retaining wall, about three feet high; above the wall, nestled in the hillside, Nash Winters indicated the swimming pool and guest quarters and then almost in passing mentioned the aviary.

"I love birds," said Martha. "No pun intended. What kind do you have?"

"The usuals: cockatiels, love birds." He turned to face her. "Oh, I get it. That's funny," he said. In the minute or two it had taken to get to this spot from the front of the house, Nash Winters had steadily slurped his drink and he took a final swallow now, emptying the tumbler. "The greenhouse inside has yellow nape Amazon parrots and an African gray too," he said. He glanced to the upper storey. "We've had a real soaking today. Let's continue the tour later and go inside. I'm ready for a refill, and you don't even have a cocktail yet."

Nash Winters walked toward a glass-enclosed, circular room that extended out into the yard from the main part of the house. "Ahead is the dining room," he said. He stopped short of the extension, at the covered stoop at the back of the residence, opened the door and waited for Martha to go inside. The paneled room, with a stone fireplace at one end, had wooden benches and hooks on the walls for coats, and there were several pairs of riding boots in the corner. "And, obviously, this is the mudroom," he said. Without hesitation he crossed the space and opened a second door, one of two leading to the main part of the house, and held it open as well. Martha stepped into a large kitchen with slate floors and granite-topped cabinets, and was greeted by two enormous black dogs that ran over from the other side of the room.

"Oh, how magnificent," said Martha.

"That's Shaquille and Oprah," said Nash Winters. "Be careful. Newfoundlands are notorious droolers."

Alain St. Germain came into the kitchen from the other side of the house, carrying several boxes that he set on a desk by the door. Martha didn't see the wrapped tea set among these packages either. "Where is Lucy?" said Alain St. Germain. "Why does she leaving the dogs in the house?"

"I let them in," said Nash Winters. "I sent her home. I'm making my beer burgers." He turned away from Martha and the assistant to refill his glass from a bottle on the countertop. "Alain, did you stop at Clifford's while you were in town?"

"I stop. He no home." Nash Winters wheeled and stared at Alain St. Germain whose expression could most accurately be described as a smirk. "Relax," he said, at last. "I see him."

"What can I get you, Martha Simmons?" said Nash Winters, turning to her. "I'm having whiskey and soda."

The dogs hovered around her feet, sniffing her ankles and leopard-strapped shoes, then simultaneously shook themselves, depositing several strings of slobber on her linen dress. "Do you have white wine?" said Martha.

"Alain, would you check in the cellar for some—" He turned to Martha. "Pinot Grigio?" She nodded. "And you can put Shaq and Oprah back in the garage."

"Oh, no, not on my account," said Martha.

"Hello. Excuse me, please. I'll have a whiskey," said Alain St. Germain. He spun around to face the desk again and made a show of organizing the parcels, stacking the smaller ones on top of the large ones, before he took two dog biscuits from a jar on the desktop and called the animals. He opened the door, enticed the Newfoundlands through it with the treats and stomped out of the kitchen, slamming the door behind him.

"Is he all right?" said Martha.

"Let's go into the Great Room and get better acquainted, shall we?" said Nash Winters.

The first thing she noticed was the Steinway Grand piano with raised lid in the corner, just inside the room. It occupied the perfect spot in the room, enabling the pianist to peer over the keyboard and strings, through a wall of French doors, to a view of the front driveway and pastures spreading below. Another ceiling-high stone fireplace dominated the wall parallel to the doors, and all remaining wall space was covered with artwork and built-in shelving: crammed with vases, glassware, pewter steins, photographs—and bronze sculptures of horses, some with riders in cowboy gear, which in Martha's opinion though vulgar were most probably genuine Frederick Remingtons. Nash Winters gestured to the overstuffed leather chair with ottoman, flanking the fireplace. Make yourself comfortable," he said, sitting in the matching chair adjacent at the other end of the hearth. Nash Winters still hadn't removed his sunglasses, and Martha began to think that he had some problem with his vision. Perhaps his eyes were acutely sensitive to light.

"Do you play?" Martha gestured to the Steinway.

Nash Winter shook his head. "Unfortunately, no," he said. "You're not from Chicago, are you Martha?"

"I grew up in a small town in Ohio. My father was a teacher. And you? Did you grow up here?" said Martha.

"A teacher. I thought either that or a preacher's daughter," said Nash Winters, smiling. "Do you mind if I smoke? I'll let some fresh air in," he said, getting up and striding to the French doors. "I love the smell of the air after the rain."

"A preacher?" said Martha.

The hinges on the kitchen door squeaked with a metallic urgency and Martha glanced over as Alain St. Germain entered with an uncorked bottle of red wine and a single piece of crystal stemware. He came over and set the bottle and glass on the table with the Tiffany lamp, next to Martha's chair.

"What did you do with the package from Clifford's?" said Nash Winters.

Alain St. Germain gripped the wineglass at the stem with his thumb and index finger, held it up to the light, and twirled it to examine for water spots or smudges. "I bring Cabernet," he said to Martha as he checked the glass. "Is important to have the robust wine with the meat." When satisfied that the crystal wasn't blemished, he filled the glass and then looked at Nash Winters. "On the desk," he said. "So. Are you cooking the famous beer burgers or what?"

"Excuse me, Miss Martha," said Nash Winters, standing.

"May I help?" said Martha.

"On the desk in the kitchen or on the desk in the study?" said Nash Winters.

Alain St. Germain set the wine bottle down hard on the table. "On the desk in the kitchen," he said.

With Nash Winters already crossing the room, Alain St. Germain turned to follow. They met at the doorway and struggled to determine who would enter the kitchen first and when, after a few false starts with body checks and shoulder slams, both men had closed the door behind them leaving Martha alone in the room, she sat quietly and drank her Cabernet. She surveyed the room for several minutes. Not a sound from inside or outside the house. She took another sip, got up and went to the bookcases. So many collectibles competed for space on the shelves, but one piece in particular caught her eye: a cast bronze of a goat reclining on a hillside. Martha picked it up and turned it over and tried to read the etched signature. She was fairly certain that the goat was French, probably late Nineteenth Century.

After she put the bronze back, she noticed the small plate on the shelf just above. She picked it up. The commemorative piece had the exact colors and depiction of Victoria and Albert that Nash Winters had described that day in her shop. But this, for all she could tell, had never had been broken. She held it close and turned it over in her hands. If it had been shattered as badly as he had said, Martha doubted that it could have been repaired so expertly. She heard the door from the kitchen and turned again to see Alain St. Germain framed in the doorway.

"I am making the beer burgers," he said. "Do you like the pasta salad or the green salad?"

"Green salad will be fine," said Martha. Alain St. Germain made as if to leave, then turned and stood silently, scrutinizing her. "You're sure I can't help," she said.

"Why do you wearing your hair that way? It makes you look like a dog," said Alain St. Germain.

Not since college, on those infrequent trips back home for the weekend, when she listened to her mother's comments about her weight, her clothes, her makeup, her use of inappropriate slang, and her father's interrogation regarding her social life (meaning sex), had she suffered such blatant and unsolicited criticism—and this from a stranger. Those weekends and the Calvinistic resolve instilled in her by her father, more than anything, explained her silence. Martha returned Alain St. Germain's arctic stare without comment before turning her back and continuing her perusal of the objects on Nash Winters' shelves. When she heard the kitchen door close, she put the commemorative plate back on the shelf and returned to her chair to top off her wine and wait.

The screeching startled her. It came in through the open French doors, coinciding with the sun's late appearance on the horizon. When the squawking mutated to almost-human-sounding maniacal laughter, Martha identified the noise as emanating from birds and then she remembered the parrots her host had mentioned on the way in. That's when Nash Winters came back into the living room, all smiles and charm, with a fresh glass of whiskey—and (how amazing) without the sunglasses.

"Do you have your mother tied to a rocking chair upstairs?" said Martha.

"Mother passed away several years ago," said Nash Winters.

"My question stands," said Martha. She stared at him: his round face shone with perspiration. But no legitimate reason existed to punish Nash Winters. Certainly not because his assistant had been rude to her. "That wasn't funny," she said. "Please excuse me. I'm sorry about your mother."

Her host sat down again and stubbed out his cigarette in the ashtray. "Never mind. I like a little sadism in a person," he said, smiling. "Besides, she died several years ago. I assume you are referring to the parrots. They go berserk at dusk. Perhaps we should pay them a visit."

"May I ask you something?" Nash Winters' eyes, already slits nestled between puffy pillows of flesh, narrowed further, but he nodded. "How old were you before you realized that not everybody lives like this?" said Martha.

Nash Winters exhaled then lit a fresh cigarette. "Fair question," he said, "and a good one. But I'm not sure it dawned on me at any given moment. There was a time at Exeter when I wanted to go to Mardi Gras in New Orleans with some pals and Dad sent us down on his private railcar." He dragged on his cigarette and glanced at

Martha. When he started to speak again, the smoke curled around his lips and mouth. "In those days there was enough freight traffic to hitch up a passenger car and since Dad sat on the Board of Southern Railway…It came out of my friends' reaction, I suppose. Until then I had assumed that we all came from more or less the same circumstances."

"It sounds like an epiphany," said Martha. "It must have been a lovely moment for you."

"Better than being mounted by a gelding," said Nash Winters. He frowned and looked down at the braided rug. "There's a downside, though."

Martha's host then launched into a discussion of his family. He was the youngest of three, and since his mother had died (he didn't provide the details or circumstances of her death), his father had attempted to increase his control and influence over his children—though the man had always *attempted* to rule with absolute authority and was capable of all sorts of mayhem. Once, and Nash Winters jabbed repeatedly at the air with his cigarette as he related this incident, the patriarch had even hired a private detective to follow him when he was home from school. As he descended the steps of a Wells Street bar, a man in a suit stepped forward and flashed an identification badge. *I'm working for your father. He's waiting for you at home.* Again, no additional details were forthcoming. If Nash Winters' mother had been ill at the time, or if he had been too young to drink, or if there had been some other unnamed emergency at home, it wasn't revealed.

Martha looked at her watch and saw that her host had been talking (and repeating himself) for almost half an hour, pausing occasionally to say, "Are you following me?" It would have been impossible not to understand with all the summaries the man supplied.

"When mum died, I came into my own money. Money he has no control over. Now he buys expensive toys to seduce us. At present he's trying to convince me and my brother and sister and their families to go on an Adriatic cruise on his new boat being built in Holland." The muscles in Nash Winters' face slackened and he stared at the braided rug again, or at his shoes—or at nothing. "I'll check on our supper. Are you hungry?" He glanced at her end table. "How's your wine holding up?"

As he stood to leave the room yet again, Martha contemplated his demeanor: he had gone from a concert of manic conversation, his arms flailing as if leading an orchestra in a performance of Tchaikovsky, to the state of motionlessness and exhaustion that would accompany the end of a four movement, hour-long, tragic symphony. Because she was watching him, she didn't see or immediately comprehend the reason for his sudden stunning scream. She saw the tumbler slip from his hand, ricochet off of the end table, and shatter on the floor. "Bloody shit in Hell," said Nash Winters.

Martha clutched her throat. A hawk had flown in through the open French doors in pursuit of a sparrow finch. The birds soared in the Great Room: plunging, rising, diving, climbing and swirling around Martha and Nash. The hawk's wings thrashed against the leaded-glass lampshade on Martha's end table, knocking the Tiffany lamp over and onto the floor, and she drew her legs up onto her seat cushion and scrunched herself into the corner of her wingback chair—the safest place in the room—while the bird skirmish played out. The avian pair did figure-eights near the ceiling, death spirals just above the floor, then twisted and rolled their way around the perimeter of the room in a masterful display of flight control. The demonstration had consumed no more than thirty seconds when the hawk, apparently realizing that it was in foreign territory, left by the same route with which it had entered. With the sparrow shuddering in the corner under the piano and Nash Winters in the prenatal position on the carpet, Martha rose and went to him.

"Are you all right?" she said. He got to his feet. "You've cut yourself," she said, "and you're bleeding." She attempted to take his arm and examine his hand, but he pulled away.

"That scared the bejesus out of me. That's never happened before," said Nash Winters. "What was that, a bloody condor?"

"A hawk—and a sparrow, poor thing. He's there under the piano," said Martha. At that moment the bird flew out from under the piano, banked sharply and exited through the French doors. Martha turned to pick up the lamp. "At least this beautiful lamp isn't broken," she said.

"I'd better tend to this," said Nash Winters, holding his hurt hand up in the air. He made for the kitchen.

"I'll come with you and get something to clean up the glass," said Martha, placing the Tiffany lamp back on the end table.

"No. Relax. I'll send Alain," said Nash Winters and before Martha could protest he had disappeared through the door.

She stooped to pick up the larger pieces of glass from Nash Winters' spilled cocktail and had gathered most of them in her palm when Alain St. Germain entered with a roll of paper towels, a broom and a dustpan. "It will take the vacuum cleaner to get the slivers," she said.

"Be very, very careful," he said. Alain St. Germain held out the dustpan for her to deposit the shards and then he dropped to the rug to blot up the spilled liquid with several folded plies of the paper toweling. "Make sure you has no blood on your hands. What happen?"

"Two birds flew into the room—"

"Come," said Alain St. Germain, standing. He put his hand on her shoulder and patted, and took the filled dustpan from her. "I must serve the beer burgers."

When Martha arrived in the kitchen with Alain St. Germain, Nash Winters stood bent over the desk in the corner. He straightened—with his back still turned—and reached in his pants pocket and pulled out cigarettes and a lighter. He wasn't using the antique case which Martha had seen at her shop and he fumbled with the pack and lighter for quite a while (it seemed like he had something else in his hands as well) until at last he extracted a cigarette and put it in his mouth and then Martha heard the crinkling of cellophane as Nash Winters crumpled the wrapper and tossed it in the waste can under the desk. He coughed as he opened the desk drawer and took a new pack from a carton inside, and only after he had slipped it in his pocket to replace the depleted one (and after he had stopped coughing) did he turn to face Martha and Alain St. Germain and light the cigarette still clamped between his lips. He put the lighter away and said, "That was bloody weird?"

"Did you get your injury taken care of?" said Martha.

Nash Winters exhaled, transferred the cigarette to his left hand, and showed her the bandage across the palm of his right. "Good as new," he said.

"I have the beer burgers on the table. Is possible to eat now?" said Alain St. Germain. He deposited the broken glass in the trash container, hung the dustpan on a hook in the broom closet and closed the door.

Nash Winters practically bounced over to take Martha by the arm. "Shall we dine?" he said. He led her into the glass-enclosed room she'd seen from outside, pulled a chair out and held it for her to sit down. The table was set with Fiesta-Ware, antique silverware and crystal goblets; and the burgers and the green salad were already on the table. "I love these napkins," said Martha.

"Christ, Alain, you should have seen those bleeding birds. What a rush. I got them in Chinatown," said Nash Winters. He placed his lit cigarette in an ashtray by his plate, sat down and spread the napkin of embroidered tulips across his lap. "My nerves are so jangled, I've got no appetite."

"A similar incident with birds happened to Gustav Mahler in his composing hut once," said Martha. "A hawk and a jackdaw actually broke a pane of glass and flew in while he was working on *Das Lied von der Erde*. Some say that he saw it as an omen of his impending death."

"Miss Martha, please," said Nash Winters. "I'm happy now. Don't go telling one of your morbid stories." He looked at Alain St. Germain who held the platter of burgers out to Martha. "Martha likes to shock people with grisly stories."

Martha's face grew hot. "Did you invite me here so that you and your *assistant* could criticize me all evening?" she said.

"Now, now, Miss Martha. Let's not get testy," said Nash Winters. "I was only teasing, after all." He put his hand to his mouth to muffle a belch. "I simply said you enjoy telling—"

"He invite you because nobody else will come," said Alain St. Germain. He looked without flinching at his employer and Nash Winters looked back just as directly, his mouth fixed in a smile, but his narrow eyes displaying abrupt anger. Alain St. Germain now looked at Martha and winked. "Enjoy the food, Miss Martha. You come this far. You must eat."

Nash Winters finished his drink in one great swallow, got up from the table and left the room without a word. Martha took a forkful of salad and a bite of sandwich and, when she had finished chewing, said, "Others were invited?"

"Only you," said Alain St. Germain.

She took another bite of the sandwich and said, "Made with beer, really?"

"When we have a big party, then the people come. But no one want to be here alone with Nash because he get very drunk and do his *droggas* and everybody very bored with him. I am very bored with him."

"Where did he go?"

"He like the cocaine. We eat the dinner. You are very lucky I cook the dinner," said Alain St. Germain.

"How did you and Nash meet?"

"I meet him in Argentina and he bring me here to live with him."

"As his assistant?" said Martha.

"As his partner," said Alain St. Germain. He tilted his head giraffe-like toward her. "His partner for the business, for the life, for everything." He raised his glass of wine toward Martha. "*Salud*," he said. "*Salud.*"

Martha clinked her glass against his, took a sip, set it down and continued eating. She looked past Alain St. Germain as she chewed, through the floor-to-ceiling windows which enclosed the octagon-shaped room on all sides. Darkness had enveloped the house and farm, preventing her from seeing anything outside except for the reflection of the lights from the swimming pool diffusing up into the black atmosphere. Like the subway when it entered the tunnel at Clark and Division, the windows in this room had become mirrors and she was forced to either look down at her plate or at her dining companion, Alain St. Germain, or at her own reflection in the glass.

"And you and Nash were living together in England?" said Martha.

"He want to treat me like a maid because he have a new friend. But I don't take the shit," said Alain St. Germain. He plunged his knife into the dish of mayonnaise, scooped up a dollop and spread it on the edge of his half-eaten sandwich. "We make the commitment," said Alain St. Germain, brandishing his utensil as he spoke, accentuating the already-prominent muscles in his arms and shoulders. "In Argentina you don't do that to people. We are the same as married. I call his father at the office and I tell him what Nash do and I tell him I demand the respect."

Martha wiped her mouth with her napkin. "I'm really not the one—"

"Sometime he no come home all night. He say he too drunk to come home, but sometime he come home very drunk. One night he come in covered with the blood and he don't remember what happen." Alain St. Germain looked at Martha now. "I find the Jaguar in the field."

"You put jicama in the salad," said Martha.

"Now he want me to leave. I tell him if he want me to leave he can give me a divorce and I take the *alley-money* too."

"I love jicama," said Martha.

"I find out who he see in the city. He is a model, and I see his picture in the newspaper. Is very skinny," said Alain St. Germain.

"I didn't know it was in season," said Martha.

Alain St. Germain concentrated on his meal now, although he still seemed agitated judging by the speed with which he ate. Martha had eaten most of her salad and about half of the large sandwich and had finished her wine. She filled her water glass from the pitcher in the center of the table and drank the entire glass, feeling dehydrated from so much alcohol. She wiped her mouth with her napkin and placed it on the table next to her plate, checking her watch in the process. Nearly ten o'clock. Back in the city the line outside the Creperie would be gone; they would be serving the last of their patrons. In an hour they'd be closed.

"I think I should call a taxi," said Martha. "It'll be late by the time I get home." She looked up from her plate and at Alain St. Germain. But he looked past her into the kitchen and didn't respond. When he stood, she turned to see Nash Winters, at the desk in the corner again.

Alain St. Germain went over to Nash Winters and waited for him to finish what ever it was that he was doing; when the man straightened, the boy stood close and the two engaged in animated conversation for a few minutes until Alain St. Germain, at least a foot taller than Nash Winters, placed his hand in the center of his friend's chest and pushed him backwards. At that point Nash Winters pointed toward the garage, said something further, then stepped around the young man and came over to the table where Martha sat.

"Let's go into the other room and talk some more—that is, if you're finished."

Martha managed a smile. "Oh, I'm finished but I'd like to go home," she said, standing. "The two of you probably wish to be alone."

"I'll put on some music. Classical. That's what you like."

"I really—"

"I apologize for Alain's performance." Nash Winters pulled the chair back and out of her way as Alain St. Germain approached the table. The young man shot a menacing look at his employer, or friend or lover or whatever he was, and began to clear the table.

"Not on my account. The food was splendid," said Martha. "Thank you very much, Mr. Germain."

And Alain St. Germain said, "A pleasure. I insist for my friends to call me *Alain*."

Martha took the opportunity as she got up to examine her host's dilated pupils. She decided that she would sit with him in the living room for a minute or two more and then go to the phone and call for her taxi, though she hadn't seen a telephone and had no idea where it was located in the sprawling house. She didn't exactly feel unsafe but she didn't really feel comfortable anymore either. Back in the Great Room Martha headed for her same chair where she sat before, but Nash Winters said, "Let's sit on the sofa."

"I'm in the process of replacing him," Nash Winters said in a hushed but high-pitched voice as he sat down next to her on the sofa. Since returning from wherever he'd been, her host had developed the practice or mannerism of thrusting his lower jaw forward as he spoke, and it gave him the appearance of someone with a rather pronounced under-bite which she attributed to the cocaine though she'd had little experience with people who did drugs other than marijuana. "We're trying to work out the final financial details so he can return to South America," said Nash Winters. "A delicate process. You know the Latin reputation for, shall we say, *emotion*." And here Martha was certain she heard the grinding sound of Nash Winters' molars. "Since I brought him here on a work visa from Argentina…He makes such a nice impression…He's very impressive…Do you know what I'm saying?"

"Latinos. You can't live with them and you can't live without them," said Martha.

But Nash Winters didn't laugh. "In my situation I've got responsibilities…and reputation…You should have seen the way he was living…when I found him…and as soon as he got here he wanted to bring his mother and sister…Do you know what I'm saying?"

"He seems pretty sophisticated to me," said Martha.

"When he finds out I'm not taking him on the boat…Did I tell you we're going to the Aegean? Maybe you should go with us," said Nash Winters.

"I thought it was the Adriatic," said Martha.

"He's Cary Grant handsome…He's a little older and he's ready to try a new career. Do you know what I'm saying? He's been a successful catalogue model for over ten years. I think you'd get along well together." Nash Winters set his drink down on the side table and leaned forward to withdraw his wallet from his hip pocket. "I have to be careful. Alain goes through things. Do you know what I'm saying?" Nash Winters opened the bulging billfold and fumbled with a handful of business calling cards and photos until he came across a picture that he had apparently cut out of a magazine. He handed it to Martha. "*Drew*," said Nash Winters, apparently referring to the model in fringed suede leather jacket and matching cowboy hat—and not to the Palomino he sat astride.

Why did alcohol simmering in people's bodies give off such a peculiar odor? A real martini made with gin, in a glass smelled good, but on a person's breath it reeked like cheap salami and garlic. Nash Winters smelled like the bottom of a refrigerated meat case in a deli. If he got any closer and talked any longer she would have to dash outside for some fresh air.

And then he leaned in closer. "He likes to have fun. If I die tomorrow at least I can say I lived. I'd rather live hard and die young than have no fun. Do you know what I'm saying?" He struggled to return his wallet to his pants pocket. "Drew is the kind of guy…I shouldn't tell you this…But what the fuck…He got stopped at airport security because his cock ring set off the metal detector." Nash Winters fell back against the armrest of the sofa and looked at her.

His face had become a mask that no longer reflected his emotional condition. He hadn't smiled since Martha had first arrived. She stood to search for the telephone and then Alain St. Germain came in from the kitchen. "I was coming to look for you," she said. "Please help me call for a taxi."

"Put Miss Martha in the guest room, Alain," said Nash Winters. "Spend the night. You'll sleep fine here. I'll be back."

He stood on unsteady legs but didn't head for the kitchen, tacking instead in a zigzag across the room, to the door opposite.

"Are you going to the bed?" said Alain St. Germain. Nash Winters stumbled against the bookshelves, righted himself, aimed for the doorway, and disappeared as if someone had tethered him by a rope and then yanked him through the opening.

Martha put her hand on Alain St. Germain's arm. "I want to leave. I need to leave," she said.

"You are safe here," said Alain St. Germain.

"I want to sleep in my own bed. I'm not afraid."

"The taxis will not come here any more in the midnight," said Alain St. Germain.

CR III. SERENADE

MARTHA FOLLOWED ALAIN ST. GERMAIN into the kitchen and as if on cue a bolt of lightning illuminated the grounds, making the pool house visible in sharp detail through the dining gazebo windows, and this flash, followed a few seconds later by a peal of thunder (Martha counted: one thousand, two thousand, three thousand...) prompted her to look over her shoulder to reassure herself that Nash Winters wasn't creeping along behind them in a ghoulish hooded cape. Alain St. Germain opened the door, where had disappeared with the dogs earlier in the evening; on the landing a few steps up they encountered a second doorway, which led to the garage, and on their right a narrow wood-paneled stairway, which they climbed. The room over the garage, lit by low-watt floor lights strategically placed at the corners, was beautiful, but Martha was no longer in a mood to take note of the details of its decor. The house and its architectural intricacies concerned her far less than the idiosyncrasies of the host. "I didn't pack an overnight case; I have no toothbrush or anything to wear—"

Alain St. Germain gestured toward the bathroom. "You will find everything in there—or here." He slid back mirrored doors to reveal a closet filled with apparel: stacks of bathrobes, pajamas, nightshirts, and dressing gowns—most of which were still encased in the original wrappings.

"This is not all right," said Martha. "Nash promised that you would drive me home."

"I think it dangerous to leave Nash alone when he do the droggas," said Alain St. Germain.

Defeated, Martha sat on the end of the canopied bed, and Alain St. Germain sat beside her and put his arm around her shoulder. "Tomorrow I will make the Argentine breakfast for you." Rain came suddenly now, drumming heavily against the bedroom windows, and he looked toward the windows. "You are better here tonight," he said, standing. "I check on Nash now and come back before you sleep to see how you need anything."

After Alain St. Germain left the room and closed the door, Martha considered calling someone to come pick her up, but she didn't see a telephone in this room either. And besides, being new in Chicago and having been so preoccupied with her shop, she hadn't gotten close enough to anyone to ask for such a favor and what with the rain now approaching monsoon proportions she wouldn't want to impose on a dear friend even if she had one. She got up and went to the open closet and chose a robe and pajamas. In the bathroom she located a supply of new toothbrushes and removed a red one from its clear plastic tube, then she turned the shower on and by the time she had finished brushing her teeth the room had filled with steam. She took off her turquoise earrings and necklace and pulled the combs from her hair and placed it all on the vanity. Unlike her bathroom at home, the pressure was strong with ample hot water, and she directed the high shower nozzle onto her neck and shoulders and the lower nozzle onto the small of her back and she stood without moving for almost twenty minutes in the green, marble-clad stall. When at last, after she had stepped out of the shower and onto the thick mat, after she had patted her self dry with the luxurious bath sheet, after she had applied body lotion and bath powder, after she had dried her hair and brushed it, after she removed the yellow flannel pajamas with blue teddy bears from the plastic package and slipped them on, she opened the bathroom door and saw Alain St. Germain standing bare-chested and in boxer shorts in the middle of the bedroom holding a silver pitcher.

"I like this style for you," he said. "Don't putting your hair on the top ever again. You are most attractive this way." And then almost as an afterthought, "I bring you the ice water."

"I'm in an episode of a soap opera," said Martha, more to herself than to Alain St. Germain. And then a flash of lightning flooded the room, enabling her to see the reddened swelling on the side of the young man's face. "What happened?" she said, moving close for a better look.

"Nash hit me with the antique peppermill," said Alain St. Germain.

"Ouch," said Martha. She took the water pitcher from him at once and went back into the bathroom and set it on the vanity counter; she held a face towel under the tap and removed several ice cubes from the pitcher and wrapped them in the wet cloth. "Come here," she said. When Alain St. Germain stood before her in the bathroom, she put her hand on his shoulder at the neck to steady him and then she held the makeshift icepack against his cheek with her other. He winced as the cloth came into contact with his injury. "I know. But this should bring down the swelling," Martha said.

Alain St. Germain suddenly put his arms around her and held on. "Thank you for taking care of me, Miss Martha," he said.

"Just *Martha*," she said. His skin was as soft as a baby's you know what and his scent, a faint mixture of cologne and perspiration, accelerated her heartbeat so perceptibly that she felt the pulse in the hollow of her neck. "Keep the ice on it for at least twenty minutes," said Martha. "I must get into bed now. I'm very tired." She took the washcloth away from his cheek and tried to put it in his hand, but Alain St. Germain wouldn't loosen his grip on her.

"No, not yet. Tell me story," he said. He bent his head and nuzzled her neck. "You get in the bed under the blanket and I sit on the bed and we talk. I am not tired to go to sleep." Still holding onto her, he took several small steps backwards and began to pull her out of the bathroom.

"I don't know," said Martha. She attempted to plant her feet but she couldn't get a solid footing on the slick marble floor.

When they were through the doorway and on the bedroom carpet, Alain St. Germain loosened his grip on her and looked at her. "I want to know about you," he said. He took her by the arms and coaxed her toward the bed.

"And what if Nash comes looking for you? I don't wish to be attacked with a peppermill."

Alain St. Germain said, "I give him a Xanax. He is sleeping."

"The rain is really coming down hard again," said Martha. "Maybe you should take a Xanax too. And give me one. We could all use a good night's sleep." She wrested free, ran to the bed, put the icepack on the lamp table, got in between the sheets and pulled the blanket up over her chest.

"Fifteen minutes," said Alain St. Germain. "We talk for fifteen minutes and then I go to get the Xanax." He came over and sat on the bed next to her. "Do you have children?" he said.

"Regrettably, no," said Martha.

"Never married?" said Alain St. Germain. Martha shook her head. "I think you have a good face. I think you should be married."

"Thank you, I guess," said Martha. She tugged on the blanket till it came to just under her chin and she sunk her head down in the pillow. After clearing her throat, she said, "Have you always liked—men?"

"I like the women too. I like the women, but I don't like the girls; they are *estupido*," said Alain St. Germain. He twisted around suddenly and got up onto the edge of the bed on his knees. "Do you ever have a lover?" he said, looking down at her.

"In college, I—"

"Oh. Excuse me, please," said Alain St. Germain. "You like the women?" He bent at the waist and stretched across Martha to get the spare pillow on the other side of the bed. Still on his knees, he straightened and hugged the pillow against his chest. "Do you like the men too? Or only the women?"

"What?" said Martha. "No, I don't like women. I mean I like women, but not like that. I don't like women like that."

Clasping the pillow, Alain St. Germain dived headfirst over Martha and stretched out on his stomach next to her. With his face a mere foot from hers, he said, "Tell me about the very most important lover of your life."

She'd never been one to talk about herself or her problems. People didn't really care, having more than enough to worry about with their own existences. When someone said *How are you?* he meant *Beautiful day today, isn't it?* But Alain St. Germain seemed sincere, and she wasn't as nervous as before. True it was the body of a man beside her, but he behaved like a little boy— and frankly there was something rather exciting about having a slumber party. It was more than twenty years since college. More than twenty years since *Dot and Dash*.

"He was on the basketball team," said Martha. "My father didn't approve."

"He was very tall?" said Alain St. Germain. Martha nodded. "He was sexy boy?" Martha nodded again. "Tell me how he looks."

"I thought he was very handsome. He had black curly hair—"

"Like me," said Alain St. Germain.

"Not exactly, but he had nice soft skin like you," said Martha.

"Did you wish to marry him?"

Martha pulled her hands and arms out from under the covers and rubbed her face. "Can we talk about something a little less personal," she said.

Without pause Alain St. Germain said, "What profession did you study in the university?"

"Art," said Martha. "Art history. I'm not sure that that qualifies as a profession, though." She clasped her hands together and rested them on her chest.

"You should marry me; then I stay in this country," said Alain St. Germain. Martha rolled her head over sideways on her pillow and looked at him, and he smiled and stared at her as if he honestly expected a reply.

Martha closed her eyes to see. The bell jingles, the door opens, and in comes Alain St. Germain in deliveryman's uniform...no make that khakis and the perspiration-stained undershirt of a construction worker, with his lunch pail in hand. *Baby, I'm home.* Martha let out a slow breath, felt the smile on her lips, and when she opened her eyes she found him a bit closer, watching. "You must be pretty eager to stay in the United States," she said.

"I could work with you in the store," said Alain St. Germain.

"How about that Xanax," Martha said. "It's getting late."

Alain St. Germain propped himself up on an elbow and bent over her face. "I'll be back," he said. Then he kissed her, a quick kiss on the lips, and jumped up and out of the bed. At the door, he turned and said, "I miss you already." Blowing her a kiss this time, he opened the door and left the room.

With Alain St. Germain next to her on the bed, the heavy and steady rain had been mere background, but now with him gone she realized that the deluge had intensified. The fury of it, on the roof and against the sides of the house, accompanied by frequent lightning and followed almost immediately by window-rattling thunder, didn't really make her anxious though. To the contrary, the power and persistence of the storm merely reinforced her knowledge that Nature and not man would always determine the course of events on Earth.

The rain in Charlotte Amalie had been like that. The inclement weather, while technically not a hurricane or even a category four storm, hadn't actually determined events but they most certainly had influenced them. Martha was sure. And while she would be the first to admit things may have started down the wrong path that night, it was later that the real mistake, her only mistake, was made. That mistake: listening to her father and mother.

Though Martha had brushed her teeth earlier, the unpleasant aftertaste of the wine had come back. Alain St. Germain had delivered water—it was on the side table where she had put it—but there was no glass, so she sat up in bed and lifted the pitcher to her mouth using both hands and drank down more than half of the contents before putting it back down. She hoped that Alain St. Germain wouldn't return. She never took sleeping pills and didn't think this was a good time to start—despite the knowledge that she wouldn't be able to leave this happy house till morning. But Martha felt comfortable, even relaxed, under the circumstances and was thankful for that. She turned over on her side and looked out the window to watch the lightning and rain. After a while she rolled over on her other side and faced the doorway to the room. It occurred to her that if she got up and turned off the floor lights completely (they barely illuminated the room anyway) she might sleep sooner. She turned onto her stomach and buried her face in her pillow, then almost immediately turned over onto her back again.

Flinging off the blanket Martha swung her legs over the side of the bed and went to the bathroom to look for aspirin. There were several choices in the medicine cabinet and she took two of a generic drugstore brand using water collected from the tap in her cupped hands. At the toilet, next to the bidet—why on Earth had Nash Winters installed a bidet?—Martha pulled down her pajama bottoms and her panties and sat on the stool to pee. Then she blotted with tissue, stood to pull up her panties and pajamas, and went back into the bedroom, but instead of going directly to the bed, she went to the door and tried the knob to confirm that it was unlocked. Without locking it, she returned to bed, got in under the covers and turned over on her side, facing the window again; the rain, no longer quite as violent, was nonetheless steady and relentless.

She couldn't be sure how long she'd been asleep when she felt Alain St. Germain get into bed. The mattress was so large and so firm that at first she thought she was dreaming, but when he put the spare pillow close to hers, draped his arm around her waist, and put his face on the nape of her neck, she knew. She felt coolness as he inhaled and warmth as he exhaled and she heard the rhythmic pace of his respiration, but she said nothing. After a few minutes, his breathing slowed (and so did hers) and she knew that he had fallen asleep.

She couldn't resist the nighttime fantasy. What if he weren't involved with a man? At least her father wasn't around to disapprove of the darkness of his skin as he had with Marquis. Imagine what her mother's friends would say if she appeared at the city limits with a young Argentine boyfriend. They'd have to reevaluate their assessment of her as doomed to life as an unmarried loner.

He said that he liked women too—and then Martha remembered that the *gay* section of Chicago was only ten minutes away from the shop. That's what she was thinking when she fell asleep.

IV. FUGUE

THE SUN WAS UP, and Alain St. Germain was no longer in her bed or in the room. Martha had no concept of the time having left her watch in the bathroom with her jewelry the night before—but hadn't she heard the parrots screeching, and come to think of it, wasn't that what had awakened her in the first place? Martha glanced outside to determine the hour from the angle and intensity of the sun, then sat up in bed to study the room in the detail that daylight made possible. The large square painting on the wall before her was either a Jackson Pollock or a good copy of one. She got out of bed to see it up close. The swirls and tangles of black and yellow and red paint disquieted Martha, and for reasons unknown evoked the confusion and turbulence of the strange night. As if in the deep interior of the canvas she could see the birds again strafing the room—or even more disturbing—a map of neurons and currents and activity inside Nash Winters' brain as he became progressively more intoxicated, with only his lower teeth showing whenever he spoke.

Martha turned away from the painting and went into the bathroom. Alain St. Germain had climbed into bed like a child wanting to be close to his mother. His presence had comforted her too. But how repulsive and foolish it was for her to have come on this journey without knowing more about the eccentric, rich Nash Winters. She would put on her clothes and call for a taxi and sneak out without any further conversation. And where was the damned telephone anyway?

She dressed, put on her jewelry and brushed her hair, but left it down on her neck, falling loosely to her shoulders, recalling Alain St. Germain's comment. Martha stepped out of the bathroom and looked over at the bed. As a guest in anyone else's house she would make the bed before going downstairs, but Nash Winters didn't deserve the consideration.

Halfway down the stairs the aroma of breakfast greeted her. Inside the kitchen Martha distinguished the individual smells of fried steak and sautéed onions and strong cinnamon-spiced coffee. But no one was in the kitchen. She walked over past the center island, took the lid off the skillet on the range to peek at the sizzling contents, then she continued on to the dining area of the gazebo where the table had been set for three. She turned back around just as Alain St. Germain entered from the living room.

He smiled, exposing his mouthful of white teeth (both the lower and upper rows) and said, "How do you sleeping?" Standing in the shaft of sunlight, which spilled in through the leaded, kitchen windows, he looked even more beautiful to Martha than he had the night before.

"Did you do all this?" said Martha, gesturing first to the set table and then to the cooking food.

"I promised Argentinean breakfast," he said, nodding.

"Your cheek looks better," said Martha. "The swelling has gone down and it's only slightly discolored."

Alain St. Germain lowered his head, averted his eyes, and went to the stove. "I have only the rye bread. Nash likes the rye bread. I must talk to Lucy to get the Italian bread."

"Maybe that explains his odd behavior," said Martha. With his back to her, Alain St. Germain began to fork at the steaks and onions. "During the French Revolution rye bread made the people go crazy and chop heads off. They weren't in pursuit of liberty and justice; they were hallucinating from a disease called ergotism. The ergot fungus in the rye poisoned them and caused them to hallucinate." Alain St. Germain didn't move or react. "You see," continued Martha, "bread from white milled flour was for the aristocracy and coarse rye was for the peasants." Now Alain St. Germain turned and looked at her. "So, Nash may be crazy from eating rye bread," said Martha, smiling. "The same thing happened at the Salem witch trials. People were poisoned from eating ergot fungus on the rye and they thought everyone was a witch."

"Before I cook the eggs we must taking dogs for the walk," said Alain St. Germain.

"At least that's one version of what happened," said Martha. "How long a walk? I can't stay. I have to get home." What in Heaven's name was she thinking? This boy had never heard of the French Revolution, let alone the Salem Witch Trials. "I like to open my shop on Sundays," said Martha.

Alain St. Germain opened the door to the garage, and the dogs were waiting right behind it. They stretched and yawned and wagged their tails with exuberance, sniffing at the pockets of Alain St. Germain's shorts, and when Martha followed him into the garage the Newfoundlands greeted her in a similar fashion, as if now after only one previous meeting they regarded her as a treasured friend. Alain St. Germain pressed a button on the wall, and the nearest of four overhead doors began to open.

"You wish to have *cafe* or orange juice for the walk? Nash like to have the *cafe*," said the boy.

Martha shook her head. "Where is Nash?" she said.

The dogs ran out onto the gravel driveway and into the grass, sniffing in circular patterns. "You need the other shoes for the walk," said Alain St. Germain. "You use the boots of Nash." He sat on one end of a bench against the garage wall and reached underneath to retrieve a pair of hiking boots, which he set on the concrete floor in front of Martha. Patting the seat next to him, he waited for her to sit down. "Please," he said.

And even though she hated the idea of wearing other people's shoes (a reason she had refused to go bowling as a teenager) she sat by Alain St. Germain, removed her new toe ring shoes, put on the boots and laced them, and was surprised to find them only slightly too large. The boy must have seen her grinning because he smiled once again and said, "Nash have the very small feet."

As Martha and Alain St. Germain left the garage, the dogs ran up from the yard then charged down the driveway to a fork in the road where, without looking back, they chose the route to the left leading past several outbuildings and into the woods. Birdcalls, which Martha identified as from crows, jays, and doves, reverberated in the crisp, morning air, and she detected also the familiar sound of Nash Winters' parrots, joining the cacophony from their roost back in the house. She could distinguish them from the crows because the parrots' squawking gave way occasionally to the human-sounding shrieking that had startled her the night previous and had awakened her earlier this morning.

Alain St. Germain had long legs and walked fast, and the heavier shoes which Martha wore made it necessary for her to increase her pace in order to keep up. The rains had saturated the ground too, and puddles dotted the gravel road, but Martha was invigorated and happy to be outside in the country on what promised to be a sun-filled, rainless day.

"You like the exercise?" said Alain St. Germain, as if reading her thoughts again.

"Normally, the only exercise I get is from running up and down the stairs in my building and working in my store," said Martha. She glanced over at him. "I know I should make more of an effort."

"You need the exercise. You have a nice shape but—"

"I'm fat," said Martha.

"No," said Alain St. Germain. "You are not fat." He paused before he continued. "But I think you are more happier if you are not so heavy. I would like to be your physical trainer." He put his left arm around her shoulder and hugged her as they walked. "Would you like for me to be your trainer, Miss Martha?" said Alain St. Germain. He made a fist and flexed the biceps of his other arm, as if to present his credentials.

Martha felt her face coloring. Had he considered how he would make the trip from Darlington to Chicago every day, or at least a few times a week, while he was in the service of Nash Winters? Or did this indicate that he understood his time with the rich man was limited?

"With the exercise you will feel good and then you will fall in love and be married and have the babies," said the boy, smiling.

Alain St. Germain's statement seemed so heartfelt that Martha bit her lower lip to keep it from trembling when she smiled back, and moisture in her eyes temporarily obscured her vision. "I'm afraid my allergies are acting up with all the rain we've had," said Martha. She cleared her throat.

Each time the dogs disappeared from sight, Alain St. Germain called to them: "*Oprah. Shaquille.*" Then he whistled, and they would appear for a moment on the path ahead, only to turn and gallop off once more into the distance. Other than the boy's commands to the dogs though, neither he nor Martha attempted further conversation.

A forest of dense hardwoods stood on both sides of the road and a small stream, whose banks were overgrown with the bramble of what appeared to be raspberry vines—though it was too early in the summer for berries—ran along beside them on the left. Eventually the woods on the right gave way to open grazing land with brilliant orange daylilies growing in abundance along the white rail fencing.

A white hay barn appeared at last on a rise—and in the farther distance the columned house, which Alain St. Germain had identified as belonging to Nash Winter's father when he had driven her onto the farm the night before—and the boy stopped and peered silently ahead. Glad for an opportunity to catch her breath, Martha was about to say something when he abruptly checked his watch and called to the dogs again. The Newfoundlands emerged from the woods, and Alain St. Germain turned to Martha. "We return to enjoy the Argentine breakfast now, Miss Martha," he said.

On the walk back, Martha looked at her companion from time to time in an attempt to read his mood, but he kept his head down, stared at the ground in front of his feet, and snuffed his nose several times as if his sinuses were giving him problems. When the silo of the house came into view, she said, "How could anyone be unhappy in such a marvelous spot?" Alain St. Germain didn't acknowledge her remark, so she looked over again.

"I love the dogs," he said. Tears welled in his dark eyes when he looked at her, and when he closed his heavily lashed lids, they spilled onto his face and down his cheeks. And then he practically lurched at Martha to wrap his arms around her. Resting his chin on the top of her head, he snuffed his nose again and said, "I'm the one who takes care of them."

For the first time Martha sensed that Alain St. Germain understood that his time at Rabbit Run Farms was almost over and she wished she could say something to ease his fear. "Do you have any other friends?" said Martha, the side of her face pressed against the boy's chest.

"The peoples pretend to be my friend because they want to be close to Nash and his money."

"I think you might be better off away from Nash—and his money. It's clear he has some rather serious problems," she said, not sure how much to intrude. Martha tried to extract herself from Alain St. Germain's embrace, but the boy held on.

"Last night he say me a prostitute when he is taking the cocaine," said the boy.

Martha managed to pull her head out from under his chin and look up at his face. She couldn't move her arms too much, but she was able to pat his hips with her hands. Martha said, "Perhaps after some sleep, he'll be more—"

"Still he doing the cocaine today."

"He didn't get any sleep?" said Martha.

Alain St. Germain shrugged. "I don't know. I come to the bed with you," he said.

"We should eat our breakfast," said Martha. She made another attempt to step back and this time was successful. She took his hand. "Come on," she said. "Breakfast always improves a person's outlook."

Inside the garage Alain St. Germain closed the overhead door and fed the dogs while Martha changed back into her own shoes. She waited while he wiped his eyes with the hem of his tank top and then took off his boots. He allowed Shaquille and Oprah to follow them into the house and, after a cursory examination of the kitchen floor for dropped chunks of food, they found spots on the cool stone and lay down panting. Martha watched while the boy removed the steaks and onions from the skillet. He put them on a plate and into the microwave before he started to prepare the eggs. He did all this without any further discussion of his feelings regarding how things had changed.

"Is there anything I can do to help?" Martha said.

"No one can help," he said. "You wish the coffee now?" he said, pointing to the coffee maker and cups on the center island.

"I need to wash my hands after petting the dogs," she said. "In the powder room as she adjusted the flow of hot and cold water, she calculated the time that she could reasonably expect to arrive back in the city, assuming she were able to leave immediately after breakfast; and, as she was drying her hands, she saw the telephone on the wall. How predictable. Not a telephone to be seen in the entire house and then there, right next to the toilet…Martha picked up the receiver and listened. The dial tone soothed her, like children's laughter, and she cradled the receiver with relief before unlocking the door and opening it.

Shaquille and Oprah had moved to new spots just outside the powder room. Their black, shiny coats blended with the dark stone floor so well that Martha nearly tripped over them when she stepped back into the kitchen. Alain St. Germain wasn't at the stove so she peered around the corner into the dining gazebo. The food was on the table in serving bowls and platters, and when she went into the area to sit down the dogs followed her and took up new places on the floor by her feet. Martha poured herself a glass of orange juice, took a sip and waited, deciding that Alain St. Germain must have gone to rouse Nash Winters. This thought made her stomach roil and she took another drink of her juice in hopes of settling it, but the appetite that she had developed from the invigorating walk with Alain St. Germain and the dogs had been squelched.

Martha crossed her arms, leaned back in her chair and watched the rise and fall of the dogs' chest cavities as they slept. Were they aware of the turmoil and unhappiness that surrounded them?

And did Alain St. Germain have any inkling of how his closeness had affected her? His sweetness—like the aroma of coconut oil and magnolia blossoms and sugar beet candy—had resurrected her past. But neither the smell of his hair nor the product he used in it reminded her of Marquis so much as the affection. Like Alain St. Germain, Marquis had loved being close. Touching her hair with his palm, squeezing her thin neck with his large hand, giving her an unexpected hug in the middle of the aisle at the student union bookstore—and at the very moment when she was thinking about the hollow between his chest and stomach muscles and how much she loved to rest her head there and listen to his measured breathing while he slept. Would it matter to Alain St. Germain that she longed to cry openly in his arms too, and tell him of the disastrous turn her life had taken? Did he know that he represented lost youth, lost opportunity, lost love?

Certainly nothing lasting could happen with this young man, for he came from another world and another age and had a different orientation after all, but every touch reverberated through her like an electric shock or—dare she say it?—an *orgasm*.

A single staccato shriek from the parrots caused Shaquille and Oprah to raise their heads off the floor. They looked toward the door to the Great Room with their ears perked and then got to their feet. Martha expected them to lie down again after a moment or so, but instead they went over to the closed door and began to whimper. Martha finished her orange juice and glanced out through the window to the grounds and swimming pool, but she saw no activity out there. Shaquille's and Oprah's whining had escalated into agitated barking, and one of them, the slightly smaller one—Martha decided that it was Oprah—turned its head to look at her, as if to say, *Open the door.*

"What is it, Oprah?" said Martha. Shaquille kept barking, but Oprah came over to Martha. The dog took Martha's forearm in its mouth and pulled, as if to coax her from her seat. Martha stood. Now the dogs barked with such ferocity that she wanted to cover her ears. Not sure that the animals were even allowed in that part of the house, she hesitated for a moment before going to the door and pushing it open to allow the Newfoundlands to bolt through it.

Martha followed the dogs into the room with caution just as Alain St. Germain entered from the opposite side. His eyes were open wide, his jaw clamped shut and, judging from the florid flush of his complexion, he'd been crying again. His tank top had been ripped too: one strap had been torn at the seam so that the material fell off his shoulder and flopped down onto his stomach, exposing the right side of his chest. Shaquille and Oprah ran to him and sniffed his legs and bare feet then ran over to the French doors leading outside. Looking first at the boy and then back at Martha they renewed their barking. Alain St. Germain put his hands to his face and began to sob. "Something terrible, Miss Martha," he said. "Something terrible."

"What?" Martha said. She went to the French doors and looked outside. Seeing nothing, she looked back at Alain St. Germain and said, "Don't tell me Nash misplaced his sunglasses?"

Alain St. Germain pumped at the air in front of him with clenched fists. "In the tower—"

"Is he all right?" said Martha.

Alain St. Germain contorted his face and shook his head. "Nash have accident."

With the dogs barking in a steady cadence and the boy now hysterical, Martha was almost afraid to question further. "Did he overdose?" she said. "Is he in the bedroom?"

Alain St. Germain shook his head. "No, no, no. Is worse," said the boy, moaning. "*Nash intentó cerrar la ventana en la torre...y él caminó en la repisa, e intenté engatusarlo abajo...pero él se deslizó y se cayó fuera* window *sobre la tierra*," he said.

It was all quite unintelligible to Martha of course. And even if she were able to speak Spanish, it would have been nearly impossible to understand Alain St. Germain through all his sobbing and choking and labored breathing. The only bit of information she did obtain from his frenetic discourse was the fact that he mentioned the tower and something about the window. He kept looking over to the French doors and the dogs while he spoke. "Is Nash in the tower?" said Martha. Alain St. Germain shook his head. "Then he's outside?" The boy nodded, and Martha moved toward the French doors.

"No. Don't go," said Alain St. Germain.

Martha opened the doors and followed the dogs onto the stone terrace and down the walk that circumnavigated the silo foundation. Alain St. Germain lagged behind.

Up ahead at a bend in the path, Shaquille and Oprah sniffed at Nash Winters' naked body, which lay in a patch of ground cover at the perimeter of the walkway. Martha covered the remaining distance in three strides and crouched next to the inert figure. As if Nash Winters had been catapulted into this position from a great distance, he lay positioned on the front side of his body with his legs splayed, one arm bent in and under his chest, the other outstretched and reaching for the trunk of the recently-planted maple sapling a few feet in front of him. The crown of his head and one cheek had actually sunk into the dirt; the other cheek and his chin angled up to the sky. Martha got close to his slack face. "Nash, can you hear me?" she said. Nash Winters was greenish gray in color, as if all blood had been drained from his body. Martha knew nothing about CPR; she didn't know if the man was alive for that matter, but she did recall hearing that one should not attempt to move a person after an accident.

Martha put her palm close to Nash Winters' nose. "He's breathing," she said. She looked up at Alain St. Germain, who made the sign of the cross. "Call the Fire Department," she said, "or 9-1-1." As the boy headed back into the house, she yelled. "Then bring a blanket to cover him with."

Martha kept talking to Nash Winters, saying his name and touching his cold forehead. As if they understood the gravity of the situation, Shaquille sat close by, watching, and Oprah lay down next to the body. Nash Winters wasn't completely naked. He wore a slipper—a royal blue suede men's pump, with gold embroidering on the toe—though his other foot was bare. Martha surveyed the area and saw the matching slipper, wedged upside down in the low branches of the nearby maple sapling. There was only one window on this side of the silo tower—on what appeared to be the third level—and it was open. She hadn't been inside the tower section of the house and didn't know what was behind this opening, but if Nash Winters had fallen from this height he was lucky to have landed on this patch of mulch and ground cover rather than on the stone steppingstones.

She spoke to Nash Winters as if he were conscious. And she waited. It seemed a long time before Alain St. Germain returned, which only exacerbated her feelings of helplessness in the interim. Martha took the blanket from the boy. "Did you call?" she said.

"He stand in the window, and I try to stopping him," said Alain St. Germain.

Martha unfolded the comforter and spread it over her host's pale body. Nash Winters was heavier than she had imagined: his lower back and sides were ringed with fat, but the muscles of his butt were shriveled and shapeless. She had no idea whether or not this man on the ground before her would live. It was selfish of her, she knew, to be grateful that he wasn't someone for whom she felt an emotional connection; and even though she tried to push the idea from her head, she realized that her real sympathy and concern was for Alain St. Germain, not Nash Winters. Martha sat next to the body. She put her hand on Nash Winters' head and smoothed his hair. Alain St. Germain stood looking down, as if afraid to get too close. He had stopped crying, but his face was red and the skin around his eyes was swollen.

"He be all right? He be all right?" Alain St. Germain's comment sounded like a declarative statement, but his tone made it a question.

"I don't know," said Martha. And then she heard the sirens in the distance. "You'd better go inside and change your shirt," she said to Alain St. Germain.

ᘓ V. FINALE

NASH WINTERS HAD BEEN RIGHT about one thing. It was an absurd likeness of Prince Albert. Martha held the ceramic plate in the shaft of sunlight. His barrel chest and round hips brought to mind biological nomenclature: thorax, spiracles, tympanum; and the ovoid head—with compound eyes and proboscis—attached to the body by an elongated neck only confirmed it. This was not the portrait of a prince; this was the caricature of an insect. And Victoria's expression, more quizzical in nature than adoring, as if she too thought her consort looked like a bug.

Martha returned the commemorative plate to the side drawer of her roll top desk and took a sip of her tea. Just days after her weekend at Rabbit Run Farms—and by the time she'd gotten back in the city late Sunday night, or to be precise early Monday morning, it had become a weekend—she'd come down with a summer cold. True, the weather had alternated of late from relentless rain to sunshine and clear skies and then to rain again, and that no doubt had been a contributing factor, but in Martha's opinion the stress was what had made her ill. Not only had Nash Winters stolen a weekend from her, but he had also made her sick.

Each time Martha coughed, her temples throbbed. If she kept her mouth open when she coughed though, it lessened the pain somewhat. She unwrapped a honey-lemon lozenge and put it on her tongue and took another sip of her Echinacea tea. That

Nash winters had survived amazed her. According to the doctor he had broken bones in his back, both legs and one arm; he had cracked several ribs; and he had completely crushed one foot. His spine was intact, and he would heal, but his rehabilitation would be a long and painful process.

She had called the hospital every day to check on his status and progress, but she had never actually been able to speak with Nash Winters. On Friday she'd been told by directory assistance that he'd been released. And Martha hadn't heard from Alain St. Germain since he dropped her off at 3 A.M. last Monday morning.

In the aftermath of the accident she'd initially been relieved to be home, away from the turmoil of Nash Winters' life. The first morning she tried to get a few hours of sleep before the sun came up, but it was futile. Her head was awash with images of the absurd drama. She hadn't slept Monday night or Tuesday night either, waking every few hours as if she had consumed too much caffeine. By Wednesday she felt the first symptoms of illness: soreness at the back of her throat when she swallowed, and on Thursday her sinus passages were so inflamed and swollen that breathing through her nose was impossible. Friday the whole thing migrated to her chest and the hacking cough started.

Martha sat at her desk, lacking the energy to move invoices from one stack to the other. She stared through the window to the street outside. On WFMT the announcer discussed at great length the pounding rhythms and grating dissonances of Stravinsky's *Firebird Suite*, set to follow in a recording by Georg Solti and the Chicago Symphony after a short commercial break. During the week she'd been comforted by recollections of the time spent with Alain St. Germain, but now, exactly a week after he had come into the shop to pick her up in the limousine, Martha had difficulty recalling the features of his face.

Saturdays had been busy all summer, and by noon she had had more than a dozen customers and two sales. A first edition copy of *The Good Earth*, signed by Pearl Buck, sold to a woman who had undergone one too many nose jobs, and the metal cast billiken bank, with GOOD LUCK impressed into the base, sold to a man, who said he was visiting from Virginia. Perhaps it would bring him luck.

Alain St. Germain understood how she had yearned to be a mother. As a girl Martha had occupied herself with dolls with such exclusivity and urgency that her mother would sometimes hide them from her. "Wouldn't you like to draw or play with your new coloring book?" she would say—in an attempt to encourage other interests. When older, Martha suspected that the woman wouldn't have been satisfied unless her daughter had become the modern day equivalent of Marie Curie or Madeleine Albright. Art history had been a compromise of sorts. Her mother had envisioned Fashion or Interior Design, but Martha had agreed to attend Cincinnati's College of Design to meet a man, who would rescue her from her parents.

Early in the afternoon the skies clouded over. The rain came later, gradually at first, but by five o'clock heavy enough to discourage even the hardiest of shoppers. Martha had decided to close, go upstairs and get into bed when the shop door jingled again. She looked up to see Alain St. Germain standing in the entryway. Rain had soaked his black wavy hair; water ran down his face onto his neck and shoulders; and his white linen shirt, drenched and nearly transparent, clung to his wet body. Suddenly Martha was aware of how the amber light inside her shop contrasted with the somber gray from outside, with both Alain St. Germain and her frozen in position like figures in an Edward Hopper painting.

Martha pushed her chair back from the desk. "You don't have an umbrella," she said, standing. "Let me get me you a towel."

"No, is all right; I cannot be here but for a little time," said Alain St. Germain. Martha inhaled to keep from coughing again. "What happen?" he said. "*No vocecita?*" Alain St. Germain indicated his throat with his fingers. You have the *grippe?*"

Martha succumbed now to a fit of coughing. When finished she took a tissue from the box on the desk and blew her nose. "Is Nash all right?" she said.

Alain St. Germain remained at the front of the store, just inside the doorway. "Nash at the farm. I have to see his friend and he live very close to you so I stop to say you goodbye," said Alain St. Germain.

Martha stepped away from her desk and chair. "If you need a place to stay or a part-time job, I could help. I know you don't want to go back to Argentina," she said.

Alain St. Germain furrowed his brow for a moment. "We go to London, England. Nash want to stay in London for the treatment," said the boy, all at once smiling and bright. "He must be in the wheelchair for one year or more."

"What happened to his friend on the horse?" said Martha. They faced each other down the aisle of the shop, at least twenty feet apart, because Alain St. Germain still hadn't moved off of his original mark. The boy averted his eyes and ran his hand along the surface of the Chippendale sideboard.

"I am the one who take the best care of Nash," he said, now looking at her. Defiance tinged his voice.

"And who will take care of you?"

"You no understand. Me and Nash have the commitment," said Alain St. Germain. He crossed his arms over his chest and lowered his head.

"What you need is an employment contract," said Martha.

"I must go," said Alain St. Germain. He made as if to leave then turned to face her. He opened his mouth, let out a long breath, then looked down to pick at something on the back of his hand. In a voice barely-audible, he said, "Can I have a hug?"

The Romans, Martha had read, skewered wings into the backs of Christian babies and swung them from the roof of the Coliseum on long ropes. Living cherubs for their entertainment. She moved back in between her desk and chair. "I have a cold," she said.

Alain St. Germain looked down at his feet. After a long pause, he said, "I am sorry, Miss Martha." Turning then, he opened the door.

"Good luck, Alain," said Martha.

The boy went out into the rain, and the door jingled shut. For a second, she thought about going onto the sidewalk to call him back. If only they could talk in earnest for a while—so that she could tell him how differently he will see things in a few years. Then they could hug *goodbye*. But Alain St. Germain didn't know about history. Too bad for him that Nash Winters had lived.

He didn't know about tubal pregnancies either. How the fetus sometimes developed in the Fallopian tube instead of the uterus where it belonged, and how for some women there was no medical treatment or surgical option, other than to remove the unborn and tie off the tube. Alain St. Germain didn't know a lot of things. She had pleaded with the doctors. "Can't you please just put the baby where he belongs?"

Martha sat down and rolled forward in the chair. She opened the desk and took out the Victoria and Albert commemorative saucer. She turned it over, held it close to examine it yet one more time. She ran a finger along the circumference searching for hairline cracks or fractures, swept her thumb across the entire surface, front and back, in an effort to detect any raised or depressed areas, and then held it under the lamp to check for discrepancies in coloration. A museum-quality restoration involved filling in fractures, mending with porcelain putty, sanding, repainting, and reglazing. But even then a specialist could tell when something had been damaged. Nash Winters probably wouldn't even open the package containing the Czecho-Slovakian tea set. If he remembered it at all, he'd no doubt tell people that a friend had thrown it out of a window and smashed it into a million pieces.

That morning after the storm in St. Thomas with Marquis, on the north side of the island, a mated pair of ducks ran into the path of their car and, before he had a chance to react, both had been crushed by the front and rear tires. Marquis pulled over, and Martha jumped from the front seat and ran back down the road. The female lay disemboweled and instantly dead—her egg intact in a pile of blue-green matter—but the mangled male, thrown a few yards away, was still alive, his head moving from side to side as if searching for his companion. "Don't let him suffer," she said. "Do something, please," she said to Marquis. But her lover just stood there, speechless and stunned-looking. Martha brought her foot down hard on the bird's neck to end its misery. Then she dragged them, first the female and next the male, to a spot beside the road where she entwined them side-by-side in the soft grass. She didn't think ducks mated for life as swans did, but she knew that if one or the other had survived it would have grieved.

About the Author

RONALD ALEXANDER is also the author of the novels The *Final Audit, Below 200* and *The War on Dogs*. His fiction and poetry have appeared in many journals including *Confrontation, The James White Review* and *The Chattahoochee Review*. His work also has been featured on Word Theatre. He is on the faculty at the UCLA Extension and lives in Los Angeles.

Acknowledgements

For "Tilden and Dewey," I am indebted to Captain Carol Wooley for her assistance in helping me flesh out the aviation details and to Chuck Rosenthal for his comments and critique of the original manuscript.

For "A Romanze for Martha," I thank Andrew Martin, for his suggestions, and my sister Teresa Branda and her friends for reading an early draft and helping me to inhabit the character of Martha.

My thanks to Jeff Klayman for his invaluable commentary. And as always my thanks to my editor and friend Ian Wilson.

"A Romanze for Martha" was a finalist
in the St. Andrews Press novella competition.

www.ingramcontent.com/pod-product-compliance
Lightning Source LLC
Chambersburg PA
CBHW030531020726
47494CB00004B/1314